SoulFate

J. THOMPSON

Cover by: Jada D'Lee Designs

Edited by: Dedicated to Ink - Elisa Goodman

ISBN: 978-0-9956662-1-4

Prologue

"Grandma, tell me again about the special ladies that looked after the gods."

Grandma Rosa sat in the bright pink overstuffed chair in her living room and tucked Sonia more into her side. The eight year old loved this story and was never tired of hearing it. With a chuckle Rosa settled more into the chair.

"Well back in our homeland in the ancient days, when our ancestors prayed to the gods and sacrifices were made, our family was very special. For they had been blessed. Blessed with beauty and a special gift." Sonia turned and grinned up at Rosa.

"Were they as beautiful as momma?" Rosa smoothed Sonia's fiery red hair down and looked up at the ceiling as fond memories of her late daughter moved over her.

"Yes my princess, but your mother was the most beautiful of all; her smile could light up a whole room." Rosa placed a kiss upon Sonia's brow and continued. "Now these beautiful ladies attracted the attention of the gods; they became blessed and protected and as such they were chosen to be oracles. Now as oracles they were visited by all types of people, from peasants asking if it would be a good harvest that year to kings asking if they would win wars. Most men lusted after the oracles but they were forbidden. Only males deemed worthy by the gods themselves could court the oracles."

"Daddy was worthy wasn't he? He was the bravest man in the

whole world wasn't he, Grandma?"

With a tight smile Rosa nodded again.

"Yes, Sonia, your father adored your mother from the very day he saw her. Now, little one, where was I?" Sonia turned on Rosa's lap and rested her head on her shoulder.

"Grandma, you were going to tell me about their gifts. Is it true they could see into the future? Can you?" Rosa hugged her granddaughter closer.

"Right. So the oracles could predict certain things, but they couldn't see into the future for that is yet to be written. I cannot and I never could, little one, and I wouldn't want to. Our family, although always blessed by the gods, lost our gifts. Now, I think it's time for bed don't you, Sonia?"

With a childlike pout Sonia nodded and scooted off Rosa's lap, her tiny feet padded against the wooden floor as she raced up the stairs and into the bathroom. Rosa couldn't help but laugh as she heard Sonia race around washing her face and brushing her teeth before her feet stomped into her bedroom. Her high pitched voice called.

"Ready, Grandma. It's cuddle time."

Her voice laced with sadness as she called back, "On my way little one." She touched the picture frame of her daughter and her son-in-law that rested next to the chair. Sonia was all she had left now and that child would be loved like no other, she would be adored like the oracles of old.

Chapter One

"Where is that boy?" Aphrodite's lyrical voice filled the empty temple.

"Where is who, my lady?" Meton perched on the arm of the chair as the goddess of love leant forward to peer more closely into the seeing waters cradled in a silver bowl. She waved a hand over the waters and watched as the scene changed.

She smiled as a couple appeared, both in their bed, the female fast asleep curled up within the male's arms. The male was awake and watched the female in her slumber, a small smile across his lips as he stroked the female's hair away from her face.

"Ah, don't they look content, Meton? Don't they look happy?" Aphrodite couldn't help but grin. That was one happy ending she was blessed to have been a part of. There was no way in this world or the next she would have let her arrogant, arsehole of a brother tear soulmates apart. Wasn't it her job as the goddess of love to ensure love rules? She nodded to herself, of course it was, it was in her job description as well as annoying god siblings and being awesome, of course.

In truth Aphrodite had been worried that her plan to bring Arcaeus and Arianna together had failed. Yes Arianna had fallen for her soulmate, but after Apollo had killed him she thought her plan to bring him to the future had been ruined when he had lost his battle with the souls of the dead on the fields of punishment. It had cost her a highly potent love potion to Hades but it had been worth it. Arcaeus had been reborn and had found Arianna. Just thinking about the whole ordeal made Aphrodite want to sit down.

"My lady, are you well?" Meton's calm and soothing voice penetrated the goddess's inner monologue.

"What? Oh I'm sorry, Meton, my mind had wandered off, I was thinking how everything had turned out perfectly for Arianna and Arcaeus. Now where was I?" The goddess tapped her chin as she stood up and placed one hand on her hip, her tongue clicked against her teeth as she looked about the temple. The white of the marble accompanied by the glisten of gold twinkled from the light of the moon and the odd sconce of fire.

"My lady, I believe you were searching for someone?" The great golden eagle ruffled his feathers, straightened out his wings to stretch, then tucked them back into his side.

"Ahh yes that was it. I believe I have misplaced Cosmos" Meton watched as Aphrodite placed a delicate hand over the seeing bowl, her fingers flexed ever so slightly as power started to radiate from her. Bright white light filled the room as the goddess concentrated her powers.

"Son of a bitch!" The exclamation was so unexpected that the eagle nearly fell off his perch; as the blinding white light vanished, leaving the eagle with spots in his eyes.

"I beg your pardon, my lady?"

"Oops," the goddess giggled slightly before she turned serious once more. "I apologise, Meton, again, but I seem to be picking up the modern curses, I find myself watching Arianna more and more and I want to learn more about the mortals and their modern ways. But I digress, my curse was about my dear brother. Yet again he has got involved in mortal affairs but this time he has got involved in mine too." Aphrodite sighed and flopped more un-goddesslike into her chair. With a wave of her hand the seeing bowl disappeared.

"Apollo managed to intercept Cosmos when he went through the gate in the underworld. My original plan had been for the warrior to wake up in the modern world so he could help Arcaeus find Arianna, but I couldn't find him. Although he is in the modern world, just not how we expected."

Aphrodite put her chin in her hand and leant her elbow on the arm of the chair, her forehead gently touched the silk soft feathers of Meton.

"Meton, we need to go to the modern world. I know where Cosmos is but it's going to take a certain young lady and her nerves of steel to help him from his current dilemma. I will hand it to my brother, though, he is a sneaky bastard, but he will not beat the goddess of love."

"You have already got this planned out haven't you, my lady?" Meton asked. The answering grin from the goddess told Meton all he needed to know. Life as a companion for the goddess of love was never boring.

Aphrodite snapped her fingers; in the blink of an eye both the goddess and the eagle had vanished leaving only the soft muted light of the moon as it wandered across the now empty chair.

Sonia pinched her cheeks as she looked at her reflection; her hand reached out to wipe away the droplets of water that clung to the mirrored surface. She looked tired and no amount of makeup could hide it. Her bright red hair caused her now pale face to stand out as if she were ill. Her only true illness at the moment was a killer headache that hadn't left her in over a week. She stepped away from the sink throwing her useless foundation into her bag on the counter and sliding her fingers down the material on her blouse, she nodded at her reflection and then left the bathroom. Her kitten heels clicked over the laminate flooring as she paused in the kitchen to grab her travel coffee mug. Coffee her one saviour, she breathed in the rich aroma before she grabbed her bag and keys and headed out of the door.

Luckily work was only about ten minutes away in the car so she didn't feel the need to rush. Her work at the Manchester museum wasn't rocket science but it kept her occupied. Her best friend, Arianna, also worked there, they had both majored in archaeology but Arianna's preference was fieldwork. Sonia was a conservation archaeologist, she focused on cleaning and putting artefacts back together and making sure they would survive so future generations could enjoy them. Sonia had always loved jigsaws which made the job more enjoyable.

She slid in the driver's seat of her bright blue Mini Cooper and popped her mug into the holder and started the engine, almost instantly the radio blared through the vehicle. Sonia switched off the radio and winced as her head started to throb; the pain started right behind her eyes. In an effort to stem the pain she squeezed her eyes shut, the dark of her eyelids instantly gave way to an image, one of intense green eyes and a sinfully wicked mouth. The same mouth moved as if in slow motion, the words unreadable. Sonia wrenched her eyes open and focused on the parking lot wall. She was getting tired and fed up of these random images that would flash into her mind. The snippets of a person or a place made her disorientated, sometimes Sonia could lose up to half hour and not even realise. There had been times that people had actually been talking to her and she had "drifted off".

Sonia pulled out of the parking lot under her apartment building as if on autopilot and made her way through the city to the museum. She probably could have walked in but she had saved for years to buy the Mini and there was zero chance in hell she would give up the chance to drive it. The traffic had already started to build up and for a Monday morning it seemed to be annoyingly more busy than usual. Sonia sipped her coffee as she waited at the traffic lights and with a mouth full of coffee Sonia people-watched. It was a habit she had along with Arianna, they would watch and usually, as most women do, pass judgement. "Those jeans are far too tight", "I want the mirror she uses every morning". At times Sonia felt harsh but she had been on the receiving end of many remarks herself because of how tall and curvy she was. Her eyes soon drifted to the right of the road where a couple were walking hand in hand down the road. Sonia sighed, they looked so happy. Their eyes never left each other and they had constant smiles on their faces. She couldn't remember a time when she had been that happy in a relationship. A beep of a horn behind had Sonia throwing the Mini into gear and moving off, but not before she recognised the couple and they had walked past. Arianna and Matthew… What the hell? Arianna was supposed to be off work sick as a dog apparently, unable to get out of bed she said. Well, that what she had said in her text. Although Sonia could think of another reason Arianna would be bed bound. But why would she lie about why she wasn't in work this week, especially to Sonia, her best friend?

The rest of her journey to work was uneventful, well, except for the small bout of road rage that occurred when some muppet had cut her up on the roundabout. Sonia parked her Mini in her favourite spot and hopped out. The sky had gotten awfully dark on her journey and she wasn't fond of getting soaked through at the start of her day. She walked briskly into the building and smiled at the security guard. Most days started like this — coffee in hand, a cheerful greeting to Bob and then saying 'hi' to her favourite exhibit. She had only seen this when she had visited Arianna after they had returned from Greece. It was a 15ft by 15ft mosaic floor that had been found at the dig. Sources from Greece had said it had belonged in one of the many temples that graced the area. But it was the figure depicted that always held Sonia in its thrall. A warrior tall and strong battled with demons, his sword arm true as he decapitated his enemy. His hair a light brown with layers of gold throughout; his body, even in mosaic, looked muscled and toned, its colour a golden hue. But as always it was his green eyes that drew her. Intense and bright, they shone. Sonia sighed and did what had now become routine. She placed her hand on the mosaic right where his leg was, touching the artefact. Touching the mosaic without gloves could get her a serious bollocking from the curator if he ever caught her.

"Why can't I find a guy like you?" Her heartfelt words, a gentle pat of the stonework and Sonia moved away and headed to her office, she had some paperwork to finish off, a little text to her best friend to send and she then had a meeting with the curator. Typical Monday morning for Sonia Cooper.

Chapter Two

Cosmos felt like he was drowning, his movement slower than time itself. He had walked through those gates in in the underworld convinced Hades could be trusted and now look where that had got him. Trapped and fighting the same demons he had fought in hell, only this time it was in agonisingly slow motion. There was a bonus, he could hear what he thought was the outside world. Every comment, every laugh, he heard. He even retained his sense of smell, and that was how he knew she was near. Her scent of wild meadow flowers hinted at her arrival, her whispered words stole into his very being and her brief touch could, if it was possible, send him to his knees. She was the only light in his now pitiful existence and how he wished and prayed he could change his fate.

His first task should he ever escape his purgatory would be to exact vengeance on the god that had put him there. Cosmos had no doubt he wouldn't live through it, but without his best friend he didn't have anything to live for. His ancient world had been forgotten and the life of a warrior was no more.

Cosmos sent a silent prayer to whatever god or goddess was listening, praying his friend got eternal rest. His last view of Arcaeus as he was overwhelmed by the souls had broken something inside of

Cosmos. Arcaeus had been a brother, his mother and father had taken him in and given him a life when he would have in any other circumstance have been killed. For that alone he owed Arcaeus his life. For that he would fight his fate.

She had gone again, his light in the darkness. She never stayed for long and her presence was always fleeting. Cosmos returned his concentration to his endless battle, a battle where one strike could take an age. His time would come and when it did he would be prepared.

Sonia wanted to cry. No, in fact, she wanted to stand in the middle of her office and have a childish tantrum with stamping feet and screaming. It had been a long morning; all the paperwork she was meant to do had vanished and she had had no choice but to track it down. So a job that should have taken an hour at the most had taken her whole morning. Sonia grabbed her handbag and her iPad and headed towards the office of the curator. He had wanted a meeting regarding some conservation work on some of the artefacts that had been in the museum a while. This was the part of the job that she revelled in, it was Sonia's bread and butter.

Sonia stopped outside of the curator's office; his name painted in gold adorned the window, '*Dr Archibold McHewitt*'. She rolled her eyes. This guy, although pleasant enough and he did leave everyone to their own devices, could and would be a pain the proverbial arse. He wanted everything done yesterday and wasn't afraid to make you look like a complete and utter tool in front of people. Raising her fist she tapped on the door and waited and giggled — sounds of snoring, then a loud snort followed by the scrape of a chair and mumbling followed. It looked like she had disturbed one of his famous naps. Sonia waited as the good doctor scrambled around the room before eventually opening the door. He was a pleasant chap to look at, short in stature with greying hair and a brilliant monk style bald patch on top. His eyes were a kind, pale grey, hidden by his thick rimmed glasses.

"Ahh, Sonia, please come on in."

"Thank you, Archie. I'm intrigued by what you wanted to see me about. I've already posted my reports on the amphora found when we were in Greece, as well as the clean-up we did on the villa floor mosaic."

His voice was kind and as expected had the tones of sleep to it.

Sonia smiled brightly as she walked into the comfy but chaotic office. Papers were strewn all over the desk and there were pictures of artefacts pinned to the walls with post-it notes attached. Sonia perched on the edge of the only other chair in the room and waited for the curator to settle himself down. She watched as he mumbled about being unable to find anything.

"The reports you did as usual were perfect; I have no issues with those. I have asked you here because I have a new project for you. One that could bring a lot of money into the museum." The curator seemed overly excited and to be frank so was Sonia, it had been a while since she had been given a job that really, in short, got her juices flowing. There were only so many pots she could clean and put back together. Her hands clutched together, Sonia leant forward, the gleam in her eye showed she was interested.

"So tell me, Archie, what is it? Don't leave a girl hanging!"

His friendly chuckle put Sonia at ease; she always had a way of getting what she wanted from the curator, her charm itself usually worked on him.

"Fine, Miss Impatient, the large mosaic that stands at the entrance to the Grecian exhibit is to be taken down and you are to oversee the conservation and preparation, eventually it will be sold to a private buyer."

Sonia's eyes widened as he talked about HER mosaic, her warrior. Well, since her new routine of touching the damn thing every morning she now saw it as hers. She let her boss talk, her mind racing over the fact she may lose such an important piece. She had no clue why or how the mosaic had become important to her, it just had. She listened as he continued, his voice getting higher in pitch the more excited he got.

"The buyer also in exchange wants to donate some of the artefacts from his private collection, including some unknown items from both the ancient Greek and ancient Egyptian eras. He hasn't given specifics, but I'm sure you can tell they will be amazing and could possibly bring more interest to our humble museum."

Sonia nodded and smiled "Ok, so you want a full detail of the mosaic, you know this could take a while. Is there a time frame I have to stick to?"

"Yes, unfortunately, the client would like the mosaic within the next month or so, he hasn't been specific."

Sonia gaped at her boss. A month — that was a mental timeframe, she couldn't possibly do all the work that needed to be done in that time. Sonia kept her face passive. Something wasn't right, they had never had dealings with private clients unless they were donating something to the museum. For Archie to be taking money for a priceless, one of a kind mosaic was very unusual. Standing, Sonia smoothed her shirt down.

"Ok, honey, I will get right on that for you. I may need an extension on that time limit, though. It's a big mosaic." With a sweet smile Sonia left the office and gave in to the urge to frown. Something was definitely off, she just didn't have a clue what. Her thoughts rolling through her mind, distracting her enough that she didn't see the gold light that emanated from Archie's office as she walked towards the lifts that would take her to the lab.

Archibald McHewitt trembled from behind his desk as he faced the most unbelievable sight of his life. The first time the deity had appeared he had been convinced it was a dream, but now he knew he wasn't dreaming. The power pulsing from the being in front of him had Archibald wanting to get to his knees.

"Mortal, I hope you have done what I requested?" the Sun god's voice boomed through the room. Apollo had had no other choice but to come to the mortal world. He had a plan for vengeance and he would not be defeated this time. Aphrodite may have protected her new priestess and Arcaeus in his new form but he had his ways of getting payback.

Apollo watched the mortal as he quaked in fear, this was one of the only reasons he enjoyed the modern mortal world. He may not be worshiped like in the old days but those that did bow down to him feared him. And so they should. He was a god not to be messed with. He folded his powerful arms and watched as the mortal gained what courage he had to answer him.

"Yes, my lord, I have one of my finest workers taking on the task. I believe she has started immediately. The mosaic will be cleaned and prepared for travel as you requested."

Apollo nodded in response and looked around at the messy room. He could never understand mortals and their overwhelming need to possess things and hoard them. Shaking his head, he took one final look at the mortal cowering behind his desk.

"Make sure this task is completed to the finest detail mortal. If done well enough I may grant you a boon."

In a flash of bright light the curator was left in his room alone. No evidence of him being visited by the Sun god shown. Archibald couldn't stop shaking, both with fear and with awe. A deity visited him, chose him for this important task. One he wouldn't mess up. Archibald McHewitt looked around his office and for the first time he noticed the mess and chaos. He felt embarrassed that a god had seen his faults and he started to doubt himself. He shook his head and stood — it was time to make a change, the rewards of being at the god's service were amazing so it was time he sorted his life out. With a sly smile he started to collect his papers. Things were about to get very interesting around here.

Sonia stared and stared some more. How in god's name had he managed to move the mosaic down to her lab so fast? She had only been in her office a few hours and then in Archie's office less than twenty minutes; there was no way she would have missed the sound of workmen rolling it past the office.

The mosaic lay at around fifteen foot squared — its size alone was impressive and was one of the best ever preserved in any museum around the world. The colours were as vibrant as the day it was created.

A border of green and blue in the traditional Greek pattern surrounded the central image. The scene itself was a masterpiece, but what made it even more amazing was the male that dominated it. Over 6ft in height if he stepped out of the mosaic, packing muscle Sonia had only seen in gladiator movies and did serious damage to how she saw men. This mosaic was a one of a kind; never before had a piece of this detail been found. The detail recorded was spectacular — from the intense colour of his deep green eyes down to the slight stubble on his cheeks.

Sonia circled the piece, the bright lights of the lab picked out every vibrant colour. The warrior stood on legs braced with his sword raised as if in the middle of an epic battle. His foe surrounded the warrior, beast like creatures neither human nor animal but a warped combination of the two. With the legs of a beast and the torso of a man, sharp claws that looked lethal and would slice you in two. Their head boasted long horns that tapered to sharp points and a mouth full of fangs. These strange yet terrifying creatures were something you only ever heard of in mythology and it gave full reasoning as to where the legend of the Minotaur was born from. The ancient Greeks, if nothing else, were excellent story tellers. The battle scene looked brutal as Sonia donned her Latex gloves. She leaned over for a closer look: bodies of the dead creatures lay piled up at the warrior's feet, heads without bodies, arms and other body parts lay strewn. Sonia squinted as she peered at the stonework and frowned before she leant back to stare at the scene.

"What the hell?"

She tilted her head and watched as the surface of the mosaic rippled slightly and then stopped, the scene having moved, but only a little. With a shake of her head she stepped back and started to prepare the equipment she would need to start the preservation of the mosaic. She ignored her gut feeling that something just wasn't right with the mosaic and set up the platform that would mean she could work on the centre of the piece without touching it unnecessarily.

"Sonia, there is no way in hell that image just moved and with that being said you definitely need more coffee!"

She turned on her heel and grabbed the large mug, taking a deep swig of the rich liquid she moved over to the stereo and cranked up the tunes. The soothing voice of Paloma Faith filled the lab. Sonia drained the mug of its contents and threw the empty mug into the sink. Her hands literally itched to work on the warrior. She had an undeniable urge to be near the mosaic, one that she had had since the day it had arrived in the museum. Sonia cracked her knuckles in the most unladylike fashion and picked up her tools. Finally, time for a one on one with HER warrior.

Chapter Three

"Arcaeus… Noooo! Stop!"

Arianna laughed as she attempted to get away from her male's hands. Hands that had her pinned and were currently searching out every single ticklish spot she owned. They were laying on her overly large couch. The TV was on with the sound turned down, the movie played a scene from Harry Potter and the Order of the Phoenix. After Arcaeus had insisted that Arianna call in sick to work they had walked the short distance into town to the local store to buy snacks and had then proceeded to camp out in front of the TV watching movies and being near each other.

"Arianna, my love, I can't help but touch you. I do have some time to make up for."

Arcaeus'deep voice caused Arianna to shiver as he looked down at her with a grin.To everyone else he would be Matthew Carter, a part time estate agent and part time rugby player. But to Arianna he was and always would be Arcaeus, her ancient Greek warrior who had swept her off her feet and stolen he heart. His new look, so different from his Greek counterpart, had taken her a day or two to get to grips with but one look in those eyes — the same shade, a deep dark brown that held the secret to his soul — and she drowned. She knew that this man was HER warrior. As always his words made her heart melt and she couldn't help but admit she was blessed by love herself.

"Anya, baby, are you ok? Why the serious face?" Arcaeus pressed his fingertip to Arianna's forehead in an attempt to smooth out her frown. With an internal shake she beamed a smile up at her man.

"I'm fine, my love. Gods, I'm more than fine, perfect in fact. I was just thinking how blessed and lucky as hell I am to have you." Arianna blushed as she admitted her feelings in a rather cheesy way and awaited the laugh or cocky comment back. She had gone from being a very single woman with a non-existent social life with only her love of myths and legends that kept her going, to now being a bona fide priestess of Aphrodite and she had the love and heart of an ancient Greek warrior reincarnated — life was simply perfect. Arianna rolled over and faced Arcaeus and searched his gaze, amazed to see no judgment of her cheesy confession.

"Arcaeus… Matthew," she grinned when he rolled his eyes as she used both of his given names. "I was so lost before you, before you appeared in my dreams and before you rescued me, not just from those soldiers but from myself. You are my world, a part of my heart and soul. I love you…forever."

Silence met her statement. Arianna started to fidget and was about to back away from the male laying opposite her when his voice, smooth and deep stopped her.

"Arianna, my love. My life without you, it wasn't worth living, even Apollos' torture couldn't compare to the pain I felt when we were apart. I would happily battle through the underworld repeatedly if I knew it would lead me to you. I love you too, Arianna, please never doubt that."

In an act as old as time their lips met in a tender kiss that soon turned heated as they showed each other their feelings in action and not just words. Arianna, for what had to be the tenth time that day, sent her thanks to Aphrodite for sending this man to her. But in a small part of Arianna's mind she realised she should have consulted her best friend about what had happened both in Greece and what had happened over the past few days. Her last true thought before Arcaeus sent her to heaven was, 'I really should have told Sonia.'

Small brush in hand, Sonia swept the soft bristles across the surface of the mosaic, each brush stroke coating the fragile tesseract in a protective substance. Each small brick was no bigger than a fifty pence coin which made the task even more daunting. The solution had been specially formulated to preserve and protect the delicate stonework from wear and degradation. Sonia had decided to start from the centre and work outwards. Her current focus was the warrior's face, she would admit and to only herself that she had been desperate to see his image up close and personal. Even in this form his visage was breathtaking. Sonia had already figured out his height to well over 6ft, a build that had been made on the battlefield and honed wielding a sword. Golden brown skin and a face that in this day and age would have panties dropping as he walked by. Sculpted cheekbones with a strong chin and a nose that would have been straight if not for the kink that showed it had been broken on more than one occasion. Eyebrows a shade darker than his golden brown hair. But what really captivated Sonia were his emerald green eyes — they had held her attention from the first time she had laid eyes on the mosaic. Sonia tilted her head and looked again at the scene before her, a frown creased her forehead.

"I swear to god your arm was not like that earlier and his head was definitely attached." Sonia's voice filled the empty room as she looked down at the mosaic again, unsure of what to make of this new scene. The warrior's sword arm had been raised above his head, but now it was forward as if he had just delivered a blow to the head of the beast in front of him. The beast's head, no longer attached, hung as if suspended as it had been removed from its body. Blood coated the chest of the warrior and ran down the sword.

Strange, how can stone mosaic change scenes? With a shake of her head Sonia lifted her watch and looked at the time. With a deep sigh she placed her brush back in the jar, five long hours had passed and she could feel her muscles start to complain. With a smile Sonia removed her gloves and with a peek to make sure no one was looking she patted the warrior's cheek.

"Alright, bad boy, time for Sonia to take a break."

Instead of removing her fingers immediately, they lingered against the stone, its texture rough but unusually warm. A tingle started at Sonia's fingertips then like lightning shot up her arm. It hit Sonia with such force she screamed as a vision overtook her.

Her warrior stood alone on a field of battle, the bodies of the defeated surrounded him, a circle of dead lay at his feet and his body was covered in blood splatter. He was awe-inspiring to watch as he moved with an elegant grace. His sword as if an extension of himself, cut down his enemies with deadly accuracy.

Sonia was unable to look away as he performed his gruesome deed, his face set in a feral snarl. She was so gripped by the carnage in front of her that she almost missed the sound of a hoard of creatures that again descended upon the lone warrior. Sonia was unable to contain the shout that erupted from her mouth.

"Warrior! Look out... behind you!"

His stunned gaze met her own, emerald green met bright blue before he gave her a nod of thanks and turned and faced the oncoming hoard. He showed no sign of fatigue or injury as he faced the creatures, more bodies fell to his sword as he moved farther away. Unable to look away, Sonia felt dizzy, his form became more and more distorted until she was in her lab again — her hand still placed against the warrior's cheek on the mosaic. As if she had been burned Sonia snatched her hand away and rolled onto her back, her chest heaved as if she had been running. Her hands felt shaky and she felt queasy.

"What the fuck was that?"

Sonia closed her eyes and thumped her head back onto the platform, she either needed more coffee or she needed to go home and sleep. Sonia grumbled as she waited for the dizziness to pass before she got up and off the platform. It was getting late anyway, she would head home and take some painkillers and get to bed. That killer headache was making a comeback and she really wanted to think on what had just happened.

Aphrodite smiled as she watched Sonia leave the lab, poor child, she looked exhausted but then again she had been working flat out on the mosaic for hours with no break. It was obvious when Sonia set her mind to something she went in full ball. With a wave of her hand Aphrodite willed the lights back on and stepped out of the shadows with a shudder. Shadows were not her thing, they may have been Hades' but definitely not hers. She moved with grace towards the mosaic. Her perfectly manicured hand reached out and her fingertips grazed the rough surface close to the warrior's form, his body poised, ready to strike.

"Mmmm, brother, you have been a busy boy."

Aphrodite held her hand out over the stone, palm down, her fingers flexed slightly as she sent her power into the mosaic. Moments passed and Aphrodite bit down on her lower lip and her hand started to shake, she pushed more of her immortal power into the mosaic before she dropped her hand, a loud groan of frustration filled the room.

"Apollo, you cocky bastard, what have you done?"

She once again swept her hand over the surface, this time her power used to immediate effect, the image, no longer frozen, played out the battle. Cosmos faced off with a creature Aphrodite had never seen before, at his feet lay the bodies of many more. Their attack was relentless, Aphrodite watched then winced as he took a hit to the back as he finished off another creature. He didn't back down, instead he turned and faced off yet another creature. With regret Aphrodite waved her hand again and the stonework surface rippled like that of a pond before solidifying into place sending Cosmos back into his purgatory.

Apollo had done one hell of a job on Cosmos, cursing the warrior to fight in an endless battle whilst locked into the mosaic. His reason for this was still unknown but Aphrodite had really had it with her brother's interference. She was unsure what he hoped to gain by this trick and it frustrated the hell out of her that she couldn't simply fix the problem. But then again nothing in the mortal world was easy. The goddess walked around the room, she took in the organised countertops and photographs pinned to the walls. Sonia and Arianna smiled back from each side of a statue, their auras happy and carefree, except for the slight tint that framed Sonia's. More pictures lined the wall, beautiful places as well as two pictures whose auras shone brightly with love. One of an elderly lady, her arms wrapped tightly around Sonia's waist as they laughed, and the other was dog-eared around the corners and showed a couple holding hands and smiling at the camera. Aphrodite smiled. Sonia had a past, one that wouldn't be easily dealt with. She would need a courageous and strong warrior to help her and in turn he would need a female that wasn't afraid to fight for what she wanted.

"Perfect," the goddess said out loud as she headed back to the mosaic, she kissed her fingertips and pressed them to the cool stone. "Patience, my warrior, your time will soon come."

With a snap of her fingers the lights faded out and the goddess of love vanished into the shadows.

Chapter Four

Sonia's head throbbed — a deep dull ache that was centre behind her eyes. Her drive from work had been one of the longest ever. Every traffic light had been on red and she had been cut up more times in that short trip then she had all year. Sonia dropped her bag on the floor as she walked through the hallway in her apartment, she headed straight for the kitchen. Her plan was painkillers, hot chocolate and bed. Sonia hadn't felt this bad in a long, long time, not since she was younger and had lived with her grandma. Sonia sighed, she missed that woman so much. It had been far too long since she had spoken to her, never mind seen her. Grandma Rosa had always been the voice of reason throughout her teenage years and then the voice of comfort when she was at university and she had struggled through her exams.

Sonia looked out of her kitchen window, she watched the cars drive by, pedestrians making their way through the park, she watched as life went on. She waited for the kettle to boil, eager to get her hot drink so she could finally start to relax. Her thoughts turned once again to the little old lady who was the centre of Sonia's world.

Grandma Rosa had been her rock ever since her parents had been killed in a plane crash when she was only six years old. Born in Greece, Rosa had moved to the UK with her parents when she was only young.

When Sonia had been old enough Rosa had told her stories of her ancestral land and it was one of the reasons Sonia had become a conservational archaeologist. Thanks to Rosa she had become proud of her heritage but she had only been able to visit the homeland the once, when she went on the dig with Arianna.

The click of the kettle pulled Sonia from her thoughts. She grabbed a mug, threw in a heaped tablespoon of chocolate powder and added the hot water. After a vigorous stir Sonia swiped up the pain medication from the counter and headed to her bedroom and her king size bed. After only a few moments Sonia was undressed, her clothes dumped in a pile in the corner of the room, she donned a large t-shirt and slid under the soft covers. She held the mug tightly between her palms as she blew across the rim and took a sip. Sonia felt her body start to relax and even though her head still pounded she knew she just had to wait for the painkillers to kick in. She placed the mug on her bedside table and laid back against her pillows, her body melting into the mattress. With a flick of her eyes she looked at her clock, 6pm, she would sleep for a few hours, then get up and eat. With this in mind she closed her eyes and let her mind drift into slumber.

The gentle wind blew through the trees and ruffled Sonia's hair. Seated on a park bench she watched as people passed by either running, on bikes or just out for a general stroll. Sonia closed her eyes and lifted her face towards the sun, she enjoyed the warm rays as they caressed her skin.

"Sonia, you're here."

Sonia opened her eyes and smiled, she stood and moved forward to meet her best friend.

"Anya, honey, how are you feeling? Any better?"

Arianna stepped back, with a look of pure guilt etched across her face. She turned and held out her hand to a male that was stood behind her.

"About that, Sonia, I'm so sorry but I kinda lied to you." Arianna bit her lip and looked again to the male that now held her hand, before she continued on. "I'm far from sick. God, Sonia, I'm so damn happy I could scream it to the world." Arianna laughed and leaned into the male, his arms instantly wrapped around her waist and he buried his head into Arianna's neck. The male looked familiar but Sonia couldn't quite put her finger on it. She smiled as Arianna continued with her story.

"I have so much to tell you, Sonia, so much that I should have shared with you back in Greece, but I was scared. Scared you wouldn't believe me or think I was crazy."

Sonia watched as the male kissed Arianna's cheek and whispered words into her ears, the blush she stole across her cheeks showed she felt deeply for this male. Sonia's mind, slow on the uptake, finally registered who it was. Matthew…from the museum. So her plan had worked. Sonia couldn't stop the tinge of envy that struck deep down. A part of her jealous of the love the couple were showing each other. Sonia waited patiently for Arianna to pluck up the courage to continue her tale. Her words she hoped put her friend at ease.

"Anya, whatever it is you can tell me, I'm your best friend. I've got your back, honey."

Arianna looked to Matthew and smiled as he gave her a visible nod before she turned to face Sonia and continued her tale.

"Ok, so you remember that god awful date, you know the one I where I emptied my drink over that idiot's head for calling me fat? Well, after I left I wandered towards the ruins as you know. When I was there I explored one of the temples and well I think the wine and the atmosphere got to me and I found myself dancing and calling out a blessing to Aphrodite." Sonia sat back down onto the park bench, the beautiful weather and scenery forgotten as Arianna went on with her tale. "So after the dance I thought I heard someone inside the temple and I went to explore, I was just exiting the back when I fell down a flight of steps and hit my head. To be perfectly honest I got pushed…by Aphrodite..." Arianna laughed. "She thought it was necessary. So when I woke up it didn't take me long to realise I wasn't in Kansas anymore." Sonia couldn't help but smile at Arianna's words and rolled her eyes at the mention of The Wizard of Oz. "Unfortunately that's where things got interesting. I somehow woke up in Ancient Greece, got arrested and accused of peddling sex and I was about to be sold as a slave when Arcaeus arrived and rescued me. Of course when he did rescue me I was unconscious after being knobbled by that damn soldier."

Sonia's eyes widened when she heard a slight growl as Matthew stepped forward and wrapped his arms around Arianna. His lips pressed against her neck as he grated out…

"That bastard would have got a lot worse off than a knee to the balls if I hadn't of wanted to whisk you away."

Arianna smiled at the male, her hand wrapped around his forearm as she looked again at Sonia. Before she could continue Sonia held up her hand.

"Hold up there, who's Arcaeus and how does he know what happened?" Sonia said as she flicked a finger towards Matthew.

Arianna kissed Matthew on the cheek and then stepped away from his arms, she moved to sit next to Sonia on the bench. Matthew took up a position right next to her as if he was unwilling and incapable of being separated from her.

"Arcaeus was the ancient warrior that rescued me from being sold as a slave, he then rescued me again from the raging waters of a river after I fell in and he even saved me from myself. I had been having dreams of him for months before we went to Greece, that's why I had been so grumpy and tired and, well, daydreaming a lot. Turned out that was my warrior searching for me and the only way he had to contact me was through our dreams."

Sonia's only answer to this was a nod. Inside she felt confused as well as slightly jealous — why couldn't she find a guy like that?

"Sonia, honey, I am the reincarnation of an ancient Greek woman called Thalia who was one of Apollos priestesses. She was sacrificed on the day she was supposed to marry Arcaeus. I am also his soulmate."

At her words Matthew sank to his knees by Arianna and took her hands in his own, the love he had for her so obvious on his face it actually hurt Sonia to watch.

"Things got bad back in that time, Sonia, while I finally admitted that I was in love with Arcaeus and I had agreed to stay there with him, things weren't to be. I lost him, Arcaeus, to a vindictive god. He was killed in front of me and I couldn't stop it, I couldn't save him."

Tears dripped down Arianna's cheek as her eyes stared up at the sky, her memories of that time taking her away for a brief moment. Sonia watched the hurt and sorrow mar her features before she blinked and looked back at Arianna.

"So Arcaeus died and I was returned to this time, to the night I had walked out of that date. That was why I had been so miserable, Sonia. My heart was broken and I couldn't seem to forget Arcaeus. But then Matthew showed up. I know I was so rude to him in the museum that day but I was swallowed in my own self-pity. But thanks to you and you being a nosy best friend I finally realised who he was." Arianna wrapped her arms around Matthew's neck and kissed him soundly. Her voice full of love and happiness; she didn't release Matthews gaze.

"Sonia, Matthew is the reincarnation of Arcaeus and he retains every single memory. Turns out Aphrodite is a goddess to be trusted with her word, she returned him to me."

Sonia blinked, Arianna's words still echoed in her head but the blue sky, bright sunshine and her friend's smiling face were replaced but the plain white paintwork of Sonia's bedroom ceiling. Her in-depth conversation with Arianna had been nothing but a dream. A dream so stupid and outrageous there was no way it was real. Sonia's only thought was it had to stem from her longing to be in a decent relationship, her fixation with that damn mosaic and the fact her best friend had lied to her about being ill. Sonia rolled onto her side and peeked at the alarm clock. Her groan filled the room. 2am!!!

"Ugh, far too early to even be conscious." She tucked the duvet tight around her shoulders and snuggled down into the mattress. It didn't take long for her frazzled mind to give in to a dreamless sleep.

Chapter Five

Apollo lounged on his dais, his golden tanned body completely naked except for a small scrap of leather that hung from his hips and covered his groin. His skin was coated in a sheen of sweat; the only visible proof that he had been hard at work in the bedroom. That and the two naked and exhausted females that sprawled across his bed unconscious.

The god was restless, irritable and grumpy. He had been this way ever since his master plan to get vengeance on that mortal had been thwarted by that stupid mortal female and his annoying sister. He wasn't about to admit out loud that the female had well and truly kicked his ass and as such he just wasn't able to relax at all. He had some serious payback to plan and if anyone could hold a grudge then the god of the sun outmatched everyone in that department. Arcaeus may have been reincarnated but that wasn't going to stop Apollo getting some vengeance. His plan had been set in motion, the mosaic was exactly where he wanted it to be and the curator had been surprisingly easy to manipulate. All that was left was to get the girl to release the creatures that were housed inside and Arcaeus would have no choice but to step forward and battle them. In his new form he would struggle to fight and would of course perish as well as his female. Apollo smiled to himself, Arcaeus was one of those males that took honour to the next level, and there was no way he would back away from a threat like this.

Female moans filtered in from the bed chamber, in turn stirring Apollo's lust. He stood swiftly, his shaft already at half mast, hardened even more at the thought of taking the two females again. Sex was the perfect way to take his mind off his trials and tribulations and relax his body whilst he waited for his plan to work on its own. His hard muscles rippled and flexed in anticipation as he stalked towards his chamber, his long deft fingers made quick work of the ties as he released the leather cloth at his hips and with a slight flick he let it drift to the marble floor. Apollo palmed his large cock as he entered his chamber, the two females writhed on top of the bed, their hands reached and called out to him to join them.

Yes, sex was indeed the perfect way to relax.

BEEP BEEP BEEP

Sonia groaned, her hand reached out from under the covers of her duvet and slapped her palm against the alarm until it ceased its annoying sound. 6am! Ugh, Sonia pulled a face as she peaked at the clock, her head mostly covered by the pillow. Saturday morning and she was due at work in a few hours. Why oh why did she agree to that stupid project? Oh yes, she remembered, because she has an unhealthy obsession with the mosaic and more precisely with the warrior depicted. Sonia had zero energy but with a determination she only ever showed when it came to getting a bargain she managed to throw back the covers and climb out of bed. Her head still throbbed but the severity had lessened. Her plan a simple one this morning: shower, coffee — lots of — and food, then maybe then she would be ready to face the world and work. Her only saving grace was that because it was Saturday she wasn't required to stay the full day; she grabbed some clothes and headed for the bathroom. A good hot shower would help to blow away the cobwebs and get her going.

One hot shower and four cups of coffee later, Sonia was buzzing as she ate her bowl of cornflakes and nibbled on two rounds of toast. She really needed to start watching what she ate. She never ate at the same time and sometimes she forgot about food completely. She was lucky she hadn't ballooned in weight or dropped to be stupidly skinny. But she had her faults, faults that she never let anyone else see. Ones that would go to her grave with her. If people were happy with what they could only really view on the surface then she would let them. Dressed in the comfiest pair of jeans she owned and a black t-shirt with the logo "I'm going to be naughty today! How naughty depends on you" written across it in white, she had tied her long red hair up into a messy ponytail. After she had grabbed her keys and bag and her favourite headphones she headed out of her apartment.

The sun was bright and the rays were surprisingly warm, giving the streets a brighter happier feel to them. Sonia plugged in her headphones and set off at a steady pace. She had decided to walk to the museum today, she would walk to work and then once she had finished text Arianna to see if she wanted to meet for lunch. She really needed the air and the extra time walking gave her to think on that stupid dream she had last night. She could only remember snippets but it still played on her mind. Her body buzzed from the copious amounts of coffee she had consumed and her pace on its own increased. All sense of worry or stress vanished as she let herself be consumed by the music that flowed into her ears.

Think Of Me from *The Phantom of the Opera* drowned out the world, drowned out everything but the words. But in turn Sonia realised the words sent home how alone she actually felt. On the outside she seemed happy and content but in reality she hadn't been happy with her life for a long time. Her job she couldn't complain about at all; she loved her job but that was it. Other than a string of random dates that never ventured anywhere — she would admit that she had never had any issues with getting the dates, they just always ended up the same way, with her going home alone and being annoyed because the guys never met her expectations or fired her up at all, not even on an intellectual level. They all seemed only interested in her on the outside and rarely listened, really listened to her. Sonia sighed and switched tracks, she needed something more upbeat. She had to get out of this self-pity mood. She increased her pace to match the new rhythm. Rhianna's *Only Girl In The World* blasted into her eardrums. Sonia was totally unaware of anything or anyone around her except the sun that shone on her face and the music that drowned out the world. The world had drifted away with the beat until Sonia's shoulder slammed into the even harder shoulder of another pedestrian.

"Oh shit, I'm so sorry." As soon as she lifted her hand to touch the stranger in an apology a vision hit her like a freight train.

She was faced with a stunningly handsome man dressed all in gold. His bright blue eyes blazed with fury and the air around him crackled with power. His lips were turned up into a sneer as he looked down on her. He would have been a girls dream to view but his angry demeanour ruined the whole look completely. Sonia watched with wide eyes as his large powerful hand reached out and wrapped tightly around her throat and lifted her up and off the ground. She could feel her vision start to waver as her airway was cut off, his words although lyrical were laced with anger.

"You are just as bad as the other mortal bitch, always getting in my way. Not to worry, though, I will soon have that issue settled."

His hand tightened even more around her throat, his fingers dug into the delicate skin and finally cut off the air to her lungs completely. Sonia's last breath left her body and her vision started to go black. Strange though, she thought. Why didn't she try to stop him?

Her vision dimmed as her lungs screamed for air and she closed her eyes as darkness started to claim her.

Sonia blinked and once again she was back on the street; the world bustled around her. She looked up at the stranger she had walked into. His face strangely familiar and his mouth was moving as his hands clutched at her shoulders.

"Whoa, steady on there, are you ok?" His smile was warm and friendly and Sonia couldn't resist smiling back. She pulled her headphones out of her ears and repeated her earlier words.

"I am so sorry about that, I wasn't looking where I was going. I hope I didn't do any damage?" With a shake of his head the stranger released her shoulders and stepped back, he smoothed his hand through his golden brown hair and then adjusted his suit.

"It's all good, no harm done at all." He nodded and smiled again, his face oddly familiar as he turned and continued down the street. Sonia couldn't help but watch his broad form disappear around the corner before she placed the earphones back into her ears. She shook her head and then winced. Great, her headache was making a comeback and she still had yet to hear from Arianna about where they were meeting for lunch. Sonia crossed the road and avoided playing chicken with a taxi cab. She took her time as she wandered down the row of shops, window shopping and people watching, a hobby she had never been able to quit. The headache had started to pound like a dull ache behind her eyes as she walked into the small supermarket. The past few days had taken its toll. The random visions had progressively got worse and stranger. Her sleep was just as disrupted as her day and she could feel herself continue to get more and more tired. A memory of her Grandma Rosa talking to her about visions reminded her she really needed to consult the matriarch of her family. That and she missed that woman like mad. Grandma Rosa had always been able to put Sonia at ease when she felt like her world turned upside down. She made a mental note to call her as soon as she got home and to arrange a visit. It had been far too long since they had spoken and Sonia had the gut impression Rosa would know exactly what was going on with these vision things she was experiencing.

She grabbed a bottle of water and a packet of Nurofen and the obligatory Curly Wurly bar before she headed to the self-service till. Boyzones' *Gave It All Away* played across her earphones as she paid for the items and left the shop, only to feel the vibration of her phone. With a quick glance at her watch she noted the time.

"Ahh, shit!" The curse erupted from her mouth louder then she had meant. Her face now bright red, Sonia made a dash for the next street, the museum in sight as she rounded the corner. With a new determination she dashed into work. She was in the right frame of mind now to tackle the mosaic and more than ready to deal with her warrior.

Chapter Six

Sonia swayed her hips to the beat of *Uptown Funk* as she sang along with the words, her voice filling the lab as well as the music that blared from the radio. She continued to wiggle her hips as she bent over the far right side of the mosaic, her brush gently worked against the surface of the stone. The bristles moved against the image of the warrior's head and one of the many creatures that surrounded him. She frowned and leaned back and again studied the image in its entirety. The image had changed again, she was sure of it. With a shrug she bent over the image again, she just couldn't get over the quality of the paintwork. The colourful scene, although gruesome, was in spectacular condition. The reds so vibrant it was as if someone had poured red paint across the stone. Part of Sonia shivered, the amount of blood lost was phenomenal and if she had seen this in real life she would have definitely lost her breakfast and lunch.

She brushed her gloved fingertips against the surface of the stone, the solution she used was specially formulated to conserve the delicate paintwork. It was fast setting and made Sonia's life a hell of a lot easier. Her focus was completely on the angle of the warrior's jaw and how the image had captured even his stubble; she missed the small fleck of stone that had become lose and jutted up from the mosaic. The sharp fleck caught on Sonia's hand and ripped through the latex and into the delicate flesh of her palm. Blood immediately bloomed and poured from the wound and landed in heavy drops upon the stone. The bright red beads fell on the image of the warrior and spread to cover the creature's upraised arm. The blood seemed to add to the gruesome scene and made it more lifelike.

"Ouch, you bloody twat!! That hurt. No! No! No... Nooo! Shit! Shit! Shit! Shit!"

Sonia spun on her heel and ran to the counter opposite the central worktop, she leant over the sink to grab some paper towels and wrapped them around her hand before she rushed over to her work station and grabbed cotton wool, a cotton bud and a weak detergent used for cleaning dirt and grime from artefacts. She had only a short amount of time to remove the blood before it permanently contaminated and damaged the mosaic. In a full blown panic, she chucked the sodden paper towel on the floor and donned fresh gloves, a shout of pain escaped her lips as she knocked the open wound on her palm and caused a fresh stream of blood to pour and collect in her glove.

"Jesus Christ, that hurts." Her voice laced with pain, Sonia lay more paper towels over the image just in case the glove leaked — the items needed to save the mosaic. In her unharmed hand she raced back to the image of the warrior, in her mind she was already going over what she needed to do to stabilise the paintwork. Sonia threw the items onto her trolley and leaned over the mosaic with her hands out to the side, her eyes instantly checked over the image, she dreaded what she would see.

"What the holy hell!?"

Sonia leant down closer, her nose practically touching the stone as she checked the surface, a frown creased her forehead as her stunned voice filled the now quiet room. Sonia had knocked the radio over as she had raced to grab the paper towels.

"Where the hell is the blood? My blood... It's gone..."

The surface that moments ago had been stained with Sonia's fresh blood was now as clean as if the accident had never happened. Even the scrape of lose stone that had caused the mess to her hand had vanished as if it had never been. Sonia stood, shock and confusion now etched upon her face, the amount of blood she had lost should have caused permanent damage to the surface of the mosaic. The paintwork should have been contaminated to the point where she would have had to show up at the curator's door and say, "Hey, Archie, I've fucked up your mosaic, can I have my P60?" But there was nothing, not one speck of blood, not even a speck of dust.

Sonia walked back to counter and peeled off the now sodden glove, she used more paper towels to staunch the flow of blood. The large wound on her hand now the only evidence that she should/could have lost her job and that she may just be going bat shit crazy. With one hand against the wall she steadied herself as a moment of dizziness blew through her, her body swayed and tilted before it passed. Within a few minutes she continued on towards the sink. She filled the sink with cold water before she placed her hand into the cool fluid. Sonia squeezed her eyes shut as pain radiated from her hand all the way up her arm. She took deep, slow breaths in through her nose and out through her mouth. The cool liquid, now crimson, started to numb her hand and gave her the courage to lift her hand and take a look at the wound. Sonia tilted her hand so it rested palm up, the water dripped steadily and mixed with the blood.

"Oh, shit."

The cut wasn't small it was huge. It bisected her palm in a deep laceration and with every flex of her fingers fresh blood bloomed and dripped into the sink back to counter and peeled off the now sodden glove, she used more paper towels to staunch the flow of blood. The pain returned and became a dull and deep throb and made her recent headache feel insignificant in comparison. With slow movements she dried it off as much as possible and grabbed the first aid kit. Sonia wrapped the fresh bandage around her hand tightly and tied off the ends. Her gaze focused on the mosaic then moved to her bag. It was time to go, she would meet up with Arianna, have lunch and then go home. She picked up her bag and phone and headed for the door, her free hand flicked the lights off as she left. The door slid silently closed as she walked up the corridor, hiding the golden light that had started to emanate from the mosaic.

Apollo waved his hand over the pool; the image of Sonia nursing her injured hand had the god clapping in delight.

"Marvellous, just what I wanted to happen. These mortals are far too predictable." With a flex of his powerful fingers the image zoomed in, not onto Sonia as she rushed around in an attempt to stem the flow of blood, but onto the mosaic itself. He focused in on where the mortal's blood coated the image of one of the creatures and he watched with pleasure as the blood was absorbed into the stonework, like fluid onto a sponge. Soon every single drop of blood that had been spilt was gone.

This mortal female had done in only a few days what should have taken weeks. Usually for his spell to have worked this fast the mortal should have had most of her life blood spilt in one sitting. Apollo frowned, this was unusual and rare. He would have to take a closer look at this female and what made her so special. He watched once more as a light golden glow started to exude from the stonework. The mortal was quickly forgotten as she left the room unaware of the magic that was about to happen. With a click of his fingers Apollo appeared in the lab, he circled the mosaic as the glow continued to grow. Dressed in his attire befitting a god, he used his powers to shield the room; he wanted no interruptions and no distractions either. From the flat surface of the stone emerged a hand, black as ebony in colour. It sported long lethal claws that were built to render flesh from its bone. Thick beefy arms followed by the head and body. The creature stood well over 6 feet tall and it looked and smelt as if it should have stayed in the underworld. It was a combination of animal and man covered in fur. Its manhood jutted up from between its thighs, it left Apollo with no doubt that it found its job role pleasurable. Fangs so large they erupted from its upper and lower jaw and an acid like drool hung in string like formations and dripped onto the floor. The creature was grotesque and Apollo loved it. The mortals stood no chance against these monstrous creatures. He had once seen them in action centuries ago and their brutality had impressed him, so when Hades had let his sister alter the fate of the two warriors, he had snuck in and done some alterations himself. He now held an army in his grasp that would bring about the downfall of his enemies. All whilst sticking to Zeus's rule of "Don't interfere with the lives of mortals". Apollo laughed as another creature crawled from the stone, their growls filled the room. Apollo hadn't broken any rules for Zeus never said anything about messing with the mortals' deaths.

Seven of the creatures now stood in front of the golden god, their breaths heavy as the acid drool pooled at their feet, the black claws flexed ready to render and tear. With a nod, Apollo's godly voice boomed throughout the lab.

"I have brought you here for one reason, you serve me."

The creatures nodded as they swayed from side to side, they awaited their orders with a deadly happiness.

"Follow the blood scent of the chosen one, she will lead you to the ones whom you must destroy. Kill them all." Apollo's laughter filled the room as the creatures burst from the doors to perform their duty. Today was a good day the god thought.

Time for some ambrosia.

Chapter Seven

Sonia's hand throbbed like a bitch; she had no doubt that she needed stitches but she refused point blank to spend her Saturday afternoon sat in the A&E department alongside the drunks and battered football and rugby players. She had taken full advantage of the first aid room at the museum before she had left and was now sporting a very sexy bright white bandage that covered all of her hand. A deep sigh escaped her as she made her way back down the street. She took her time as she was still waiting on a text from Arianna about when and where they should meet. To be honest she wasn't bothered with the where she just wanted food. Sonia was starving and after the little accident in the lab she felt she deserve a huge lunch with dessert.

Sonias phone vibrated the tune of *Fraggle Rock* followed the vibrations from her pocket. She fished it out and looked at the screen, two messages were waiting. Sonia had totally forgotten about receiving the first message.

"Sonia, the date on the mosaic has been moved up, I will need to you in longer and every day as well. Thank you. Archie."

"Oh for fuck's sake, you have got to be kidding me." Sonia's angry voice got blatant stares of annoyance from other pedestrians for her use of the f-word, glaring at them in return she swiped the phone and read the second message.

"Hey bestie, meet me at the park I've got something to tell you. Arianna xx"

A sense of déjà vu hit her as she crossed the street and headed towards the park. Luckily the sun still shone and the temperature was still rising. The park was beautiful in the summer, the trees were full of leaves and flowers, the grass had also been freshly cut. It had that summer smell that always reminded her of summers spent at her Grandma Rosas house. Sonia took deep breaths of the cool air and smiled as people went about their lives. Running, walking or cycling, they all enjoyed the splendor of the summers day. Sonia lifted her face to the sun and let the rays wash over her skin as she walked into the park and towards the bench that faced the small pond in the park. This was where they always met up when they did lunch.

Yet another overwhelming sense of déjà vu flitted across Sonia's mind as she sat on the bench, she closed her eyes in an attempt to grab the memory but it flitted out of her grasp. With a frown she opened her eyes and looked down at her heavily bandaged hand, she turned it over palm up and noticed the light pink stain that now covered a small section of the palm, her blood had already seeped through the bandage. The pain hadn't lessened any and now shot dull throbs up her arm. That and the ever present headache caused Sonia's whole body to be on edge and in turn made her feel a little bit grumpy. Sonia's irritability wouldn't leave her and, as such, she had to get up and pace around the bench, she had a feeling that something was going to happen. It was a deep uncomfortable feeling in the pit of her stomach that made her feel nauseous. She started to grumble to herself as she circled the bench and on the third circuit a voice cut through her inner turmoil.

"Sonia, there you are!"

Sonia turned and faced her best friend; she looked fine, awesome in fact. She definitely didn't look like she was sick. Sonia frowned again as her headache got worse, the feeling that they had done this before getting more intense.

"Hey, Arianna." Sonia rushed over and hugged her friend hard, careful to keep her injured hand out of the way and out of sight.

"Oh, honey, I've missed you so much," Arianna whispered in Sonia's ears as she returned the hug just as hard. Sonia smiled and refused to give up the hug as her eyes moved to a man that was stood watching their exchange. He looked familiar and Sonia frowned again. She really had done this before. Arianna released her and stepped away and towards the male.

"Anya, honey, how are you feeling? Any better?"

Arianna stepped back, with a look of pure guilt etched across her face. She turned and held out her hand to the male that was stood behind her.

"About that, Sonia, I'm so sorry but I kinda lied to you." Arianna bit her lip and looked again to the male that now held her hand, before she continued on. "I'm far from sick. God, Sonia, I'm so damn happy I could scream it to the world." Arianna laughed and leaned into the male, his arms instantly wrapped around her waist and he buried his head into Arianna's neck. The male looked familiar but Sonia couldn't quite put her finger on it. Then it hit her, she had seen this whole scene before, in fact she had dreamt it. Sonia held up her hand to stop the marathon of a story her best friend was going to reveal to her.

"I know, Anya, honey. Your man there is the love of your life and you call him Arcaeus because that was his name back in ancient Greece where he was a warrior for Apollo, and this is his reincarnated form. Is that right?" Sonia smiled as both Arianna and her man looked stunned at her reveal. She had no idea how she knew or if the dream was true, but every word that had left her mouth felt right. Arianna looked at the male and he drew her into this embrace. The feelings of envy Sonia recalled from the dream came flooding back.

"Yes, Sonia, you are correct. Though how you are aware of these facts is mysterious indeed. But since both I and Arianna have dealt with a lot stranger occurrences we are going to put it down to the will of the gods." He kissed Arianna's head and she turned in his arms to face Sonia.

"Sonia, how did you know? I've not mentioned this to anyone because I was convinced you would think I was crazy."

Sonia bit her lip and folded her arms across her chest and continued to pace in front of the couple, that gut feeling that something was about to happen had become too intense, she shrugged and answered.

"I don't know, hun, déjà vu I guess. I just remember being stood exactly here and you told me about your dance in the temple and about Aphrodite as well as Apollo and the fact you lost your man." Sonia looked around the park and noticed it had gotten quieter, the weather was still beautiful so the park should have been filled by now. "Listen, can we go somewhere else? I'm not feeling too great right now." Sonia pointed to the entrance and forgot about her heavily bandaged hand.

"Sonia, what the hell did you do to yourself?" Arianna rushed over and tried to take a look at her hand, she pulled it out of her friend's grip and hid it behind her back.

"Anya, it's nothing for you to worry about. I just had a small accident at work earlier, it's noth..." Sonia's words were cut off by a woman's scream followed by shouts and growls that erupted from the entrance to the park. All three of them watched as people fled in all directions from an unknown source. Arcaeus, or Matthew as Sonia remembered him, placed Arianna behind him and reached under his top. He pulled out a lethal looking knife from a hidden sheath and faced the unknown foe. In his stance alone you could see the warrior he truly was. More screams rent the air and from behind a tree several strange looking men revealed themselves. On further inspection Sonia recognised them for what they truly were.

"Oh fuck, those.... those things are the creatures from the mosaic I've been working on." Arianna turned and looked at her best friend, her face full of worry.

"What mosaic, Sonia?"

Sonia pulled her gaze from the creatures to Arianna's face.

"The main mosaic that stood in the entrance to the Ancient Civilisations department. Archie asked me to work on it as we had a buyer who was willing to donate to the museum, that's how I did this." She held up her palm, the pink stain now a full blown bright red. The wound had refused to stop bleeding.

"Arcaeus?" Arianna's voice was quiet as she looked to her man, his face was set with determination.

"Take Sonia and go, baby, I will hold them off for as long as I can." His hand held the knife in what looked like a relaxed grip, but Sonia knew he would be a lethal foe with it. Arianna shook her head and Sonia saw the tears fall down her cheeks.

"No, Arcaeus! I am not leaving you, I won't lose you again!"

With one hand he pulled Arianna in close and held her tight as their lips met in a desperate kiss that ended to the reluctance of Arianna, their foreheads rested against each other's as he whispered.

"Go! Take Sonia for she is important to this somehow, I will find you, never doubt that, my love." With a gentle push he sent her away and faced off with the creatures; his back to the girls he angrily threw an order to them

"FUCKING GO!!"

With a cry Arianna grabbed Sonia's hand and started to run for the opposite entrance to the park, but not before she shouted, "Arcaeus, I love you. Blessed Aphrodite hear my call, protect my soulmate. Please."

With one last look Sonia watched Arcaeus dive into battle, his roar of rage echoed throughout the park as they ran as fast as they could. Sonia hoped with all that she had that Arianna's man would be ok.

"What the hell are those things, Arianna?"

Her best friend looked over as they ran out of the park

"I have no idea, Sonia. I have no idea."

Chapter Eight

Arcaeus watched the creatures as they swayed, their black eyes flicked from him to the girls as they made their escape. He hadn't wanted to scare Arianna but he had seen these beings before. He had fought them before, fought them and lost. He slowed his breathing down and took a relaxed stance. He had more to live for but a part of him knew the damage these beasts of the underworld could do, knew there was a high possibility that he wouldn't make it back to Arianna. But as long as he protected her he would be content. The dark creatures growled their displeasure and moved to circle him, he flexed the knife in his hand and sent a prayer up to Apol… He shook his head, never Apollo, but old habits die hard. His voice was calm, belying the nerves that flitted through his body.

"Aphrodite, goddess of love, I pray you protect my love. Give her the strength to go on without me. I ask for peace in Elyssia." With a roar Arcaeus ran forward and met the creatures head on, his knife a lethal extension of his arm, he made each hit to the beasts count, removing limbs and severing arteries. His cry pierced the air and filled the park as the black claws raked down his back, they ripped through cloth and flesh and brought him to his knees.

Three of the creatures surrounded him; the others he had no idea where they had gone and they were the least of his worries right now. With one hand on the knife he pushed forward and thrust, the knife sunk into the creature's flesh and hit bone. Its scream of pain caused goosebumps to crawl over Arcaeus' skin like bugs over a log. The creature fell to its knees, its clawed hand covered the now gaping wound in its stomach as blood and other tissue leaked from it. Using all of his strength Arcaeus used the knife and in one arc of movement severed the creatures head from its body.

'One down,' Arcaeus thought as he turned and watched, as if in slow motion, another set of black claws descend upon him. His eyes wide he faced his doom, his thoughts of Arianna and the life he so desperately wanted with her. Arcaeus closed his eyes and accepted his fate. The gods no matter fickle always had a plan.

Cosmos ran hard, his arms pumped at his side and his two swords bounced against his back as he tracked the creatures from the underworld. Never in all of his dreams had he believed he would be freed but he wouldn't snub this gift in its face. The only downside to him being freed was that creatures were also free. Free and from the sounds of things they had already started to cause mayhem. His feet swiftly took him along a road, a road that was smooth and covered in a strange substance, strange horseless carts moved up and down the road and produced loud noises. As well as this the buildings looked as if they should be next to Mount Olympus herself for they stretched to the sky.

Cosmos increased his speed, the creatures could have caused so much damage he didn't dare slow down. He entered a sparsely wooded area, his feet ate up the ground as they followed the screams of fear. Other pedestrians ran in the opposite direction, this in itself told him he was on the right track. Cosmos had felt completely disorientated when he had emerged from the mosaic. He remembered the scent of the stunning female that had been near, the feel of her fingers as she had brushed along his face and jaw. Her touch, even in imprisonment, had set him alight. He had felt her pain when she had cut herself and thus freeing him and the creatures. So as soon as he had dispatched with the beasts and sent them back to the underworld he would find this female. Find her and put an end to her. As much as she was beautiful she was a distraction and a way for the gods to unleash hell upon the world and that was something his honour wouldn't allow. Her blood was the key, that much he knew. She was special and the god that was behind all this knew and wouldn't hesitate to use her again.

He lifted his arms and freed the double swords at his back, he rounded a tree and saw a mortal with a knife beheading one of the creatures. Impressive for they were not that easy to kill. Two more of the beasts now descended upon the mortal, his cry of pain and anger spurred Cosmos on. Something was somewhat familiar about the way the mortal battled. With a war cry of his own Cosmos entered the fray, his sword quickly removed the arm of the creature that was about to remove the mortal's head from his body. With deft efficiency he dispatched the creature and turned to face the final one, fully aware the mortal had stood and faced off beside him. Cosmos held his right hand out to the side and spoke to the wounded man.

"Stay. I will deal with this monster, you have fought well."

With no argument the man nodded and bent at the waist, his breaths sawed in and out, his pain obvious. Cosmos tuned into the creature in front of him, his wrists loose as he stepped forward and attacked; the creature not afraid swung his own clawed weapons and connected with Cosmos' left arm, slicing through the muscle. With a growl Cosmos turned and used the sword in his right hand, its lethal edge cut through the creature's neck throwing the head into the air, blood sprayed and coated the grass.

Cosmos turned to circle the injured mortal, his eyes took in every tree, every shadow as he waited for another attack. He knew more than three of the creatures had been freed before him so he didn't dare risk letting his guard down. He walked back to the mortal, his hand going to his shoulder.

"You did well. Pray tell me were there more before I arrived? How badly are you injured, should I call for a healer?"

The male stood; the only evidence he was in pain was a slight wince.

"Cosmos, my friend, you can't imagine how good it is to see you again. I thought it would never happen."

Cosmos stared. How did this man know his name and why did he speak to him as if they were friends? He stepped away and held out his swords. "You know me? How? Be quick with your words or I will fell you like the creatures of the underworld"

The man straightened more and smiled.

"Cosmos, my friend, it is me Arcaeus. Put your swords down, I mean you no harm." He held his arms out to the side as a sign, showing he meant what he said.

Never letting his gaze wander from the male, Cosmos dropped to one knee and wiped the blades of his swords on the grass. His voice calm, belying the shock at the man's words that coursed through him.

"If you are Arcaeus, then how are you in this form? Tell me something only my friend would know."

With a smile he bent and retrieved his own knife, a hiss of breath left him as the cuts in his back opened again. Warm blood seeped from the flesh and stained his shirt.

"I am in this form thanks to Aphrodite herself. You remember our battle in the underworld? You remember I fell? Well, she gave me a chance to be with Arianna, my soul was reincarnated into this form."

Cosmos looked up and into the eyes of the mortal that stood proudly in front of him — that was it, the familiarity of the way he fought and the knowledge in his eyes. He was his long-time friend and he didn't doubt for a second that Aphrodite had been involved. The gods had already become involved when they, or more precisely Apollo, tortured Arcaeus' previous form back in Greece. He stood and clasped his friend's arm.

"Arcaeus, I am glad to know that the fates hadn't completely given up on you. So tell me, where am I? This land is...strange."

Arcaeus clapped the warrior on the back and then dug into his pocket, he pulled out a small square item and his fingers started to move rapidly across the surface. Cosmos watched with awe as it lit up and gave out music.

"Bless the gods, what is this magic?" With a chuckle Arcaeus started to walk away. His voice pulled Cosmos out of his thoughts of wonder and entranced him to follow.

"Come, my friend, I will explain all. I have no doubt you have questions and I am more than willing to answer them but I need to be near Arianna, I hate not being by her side to protect her. We will get you washed and fed and then we can decide what to do about this ancient evil that has decided to plague us."

Cosmos sheathed his swords at his back and moved to follow his friend. Life had decidedly taken a turn for the unusual and he didn't doubt it would continue to be...strange for the time being.

Chapter Nine

Aphrodite frowned as her priestess's plea rang out through her temple, the sound of pain and fear obvious in the power of the plea. With a snap of her fingers the goddess called a bowl to appear in front and waved her hand over the silver water. The image of Arianna and her friend Sonia running down the road full of fear gave her pause. Where was Arcaeus? Surely he would be close by for he never left her side.

"Show me my warrior," her voice clear as crystal rang out and the image zoomed to the park. She watched as her proud and brave warrior stood against creatures from the depths of the underworld, creatures she had watched him fight when he battled for his freedom and lost. She watched as four split off from the group attacking Arcaeus and started to track the females. This she couldn't allow.

"Wind, my friend, aid me in this quest, hide my chosen from this foe." With her hands raised in the air she called her power. Using the wind to hide Arianna's and Sonia's scent. Helping to protect them until she had enough power to offer more. Aphrodite frowned as her power struggled to do her bidding. Something had messed with the flow of power and her energies didn't feel right at all. She felt like she had nothing to give or as the mortals put it, 'She had no juice left in the tank.' Even a small protection spell had taken its toll and the way her power felt at the moment her spell would last a day at the most.

She peered back into the pool, a small smile played on her lips as she watched Cosmos appear and aid his friend. Both warriors battled hard and with a ferocity that she admired. With visible ease they defeated the creatures, though not all of them had stayed for the short battle. Aphrodite was pleased in one sense, Sonia had been as she had known all along — the perfect female to free Cosmos from the mosaic — but those creatures had been freed as well which was something the goddess hadn't expected. She was concerned about those beasts, after she had witnessed their viciousness in the underworld she couldn't help but shudder at the thought of the damage they could do in the mortal realm. Aphrodite looked again at her warriors and looked more closely at Cosmos, yes Sonia was the perfect female for him but getting them both to admit any sort of feelings would be a battle in itself. They both had demons that needed to be defeated and she just hoped they could push past them and finally find love.

The goddess swept her hand across the small pool and the vision vanished leaving only a ripple of water, she sagged back into the chair and smacked her palm on the arm as a strange exhaustion over took her. In a voice clear as crystal but laced with fatigue she called out.

"Meton, I need you my friend." The lyrical sound of her voice sounded throughout the room. Soon the whisper of feather wings filled the void of silence as the great golden eagle soared into the room, he landed with grace on a pedestal next to the goddess.

"My lady, you called for me" His head bowed in respect and he waited patiently as always.

"Meton, my dear, I ask you go to Hades and request the god's company. I have need to talk to him." Aphrodite smiled and lifted her hand to stroke the eagle's head, her fingers grazed the soft feathers. "And hurry back for I don't quite feel myself."

With a tilt of his head he looked upon his goddess and noticed a light paleness to her complexion and a tiredness around her eyes he had never witnessed before.

"My lady, are you not well?" He shuffled on clawed feet and moved closer to her outstretched hand.

"I do not know Meton, my powers are…" she shook her head. "They are weak, I feel weak. This is unusual for I have never felt this way before." She sighed heavily and looked the great golden eagle in the eye. "Go, my friend, and then hurry back for I am going to need your help."

With a nod of his golden head Meton stretched out his golden wings and took off in one fluid movement, his path took him over the realm of the gods and towards the entrance to the underworld. His task more important than anything, for his goddess had asked this of him. He only hoped he didn't have issues with the guardian at the entrance of the underworld. For all of his powers and skills at keeping the realm of the underworld in check, Hades had made one big mistake. Meton flew on swift wings, the slight shudder that overtook him was masked with a ripple of feathers. Hades' one mistake, having a bloody multi-headed dog that slobbered as a guardian and who seemed to think Meton was his own personal toy. With a weary sigh the great bird descended towards the entrance.

He would lay down his life for his goddess and would do whatever it took to make sure no evil would befall her. Even if it meant playing 'go fetch' with Olympus' biggest puppy.

Arianna clutched her side as she leant against the wall and panted, her words broken by each intake of breath.

"Do you think they followed us, Sonia?"

Sonia peeked out of the window of her apartment and scanned the streets below. They had run all of the way home and she now felt like her heart would explode from her chest. Her eyes looked back and forth and she watched every side street and shadow for any sign of the hideous creatures that had appeared in the park. She let go of the blind and watched as it fell into place and turned to face her equally exhausted friend. She watched concerned as Arianna had moved away from the wall and she had started to pace across the room in front of her extra-large and extra wide flat screen TV. She was chewing on her lower lip, this action in itself showed how anxious she truly was, her fingers flew across the screen of her phone. Sonia had no idea how to offer comfort that would help her best friend. She had zero experience in this kind of thing. She could only watch as Arianna walked a hole in her rug and attempted not to break down. Not that Sonia could blame her she could say with a certainty that if she had just met 'the one' and he was somehow battling for his life — there was no way she would be holding up this well.

"Anya, honey, sit down and let me make a brew, yeah?" Sonia

needed to do something, her hand had become more and more painful. As soon as she had got home she had ripped off the bandage and now had her hand wrapped in strips of towel, she hoped that is would absorb most of the blood and maybe get it to stop. Sonia used her uninjured hand to lift the kettle from its cradle and fill it with water before she put it back and switched it on. She grabbed two large mugs from the shelf as her thoughts started to wander. They returned once again to Arianna and her boyfriend. No, boyfriend wasn't the right word, with a quiet sigh she admitted to herself that the word Arianna had used was in fact perfect. "Soulmates," it suited them as a couple, it was intense and serious and the word itself just cried out forever.

Sonia absently placed the teabags into the mugs. She could hear Arianna continue to pace, the sounds of her muttering became background noise as Sonia's mind drifted off as she waited for the kettle to finish its boil. Her emotions were torn in two, in one sense she was envious and jealous of what Arianna now had: Arcaeus, or Matthew, in her life. But in the other she was overjoyed that her best friend was finally happy. Sonia had watched Arianna for years just plod through life, not really living it and enjoying it. Any man Sonia had introduced her to had majorly fucked things up and not one of them had seen past her exterior to what was inside. Sonia shook her head, there was sweet fuck all wrong with her best friend, she suited curvy and she was stunningly beautiful. Well, not that she would let anyone tell her anyway. Arianna always clammed up the minute you tried to compliment her. So finally she had a man, one that saw what the rest of those idiots had missed. Arianna was and always had been smart and beautiful with a heart of gold and wicked sense of humour.

The kettle let out a loud click and pulled Sonia from her thoughts, it dragged her back to the now. She took in a long deep breath and then released it as she picked up the kettle and poured the hot water into the cups. The spoon in hand she stirred absentmindedly. No, she may be envious, but she was definitely more overjoyed for Arianna. She now had what nearly every woman dreamed of. Sonia pulled out the teabags and squeezed the excess liquid back into the cups before she threw them into the bin. Now she just hoped and, yeah, she prayed that Arcaeus… Matthew, whatever he liked to be called, managed to escape from those things. Sonia knew without any doubt that there would be no consoling Arianna if he didn't return.

A high pitched scream caused Sonia to forget the mugs as she turned and raced back into the living room. She found Arianna sagged on the floor in a heap as she sobbed, her breath hitched and her shoulders shook.

"Anya, honey, what is it? Tell me honey." She reached out to stroke Arianna's hair from her face but froze when she looked up and beamed a full out smile regardless of the tears that still fell from her eyes.

"He's ok, Sonia. He's ok." With those words Arianna threw her arms around Sonia's neck and dragged her down onto the floor for a huge hug, their giggles of happiness soon filled the room as the tension quickly lifted.

Chapter Ten

Cosmos sat stunned in the back of the mental beast Arcaeus had insisted they enter, one he had called a omaxi.' His warrior training had never prepared him for a situation like this so all he did was hold on to the material he sat on, closed his eyes and silently prayed to Zeus that he would survive. Beasts, monsters, even gods he could face but this was frightening and had his stomach on a constant roll since they had started to move. He had zero control and that scared him the most. He had said he would have preferred to walk but Arcaeus had demanded they use this thing as he was eager to return to his woman.

Cosmos exited quickly and stood on very shaky legs, never in all of his years had he felt nauseous whilst he travelled. His perfect, flawless record of being a man was gone as he dry heaved into a nearby receptacle. In that moment Cosmos felt his friend's presence, he stood and turned, his friend stood arms folded across his massive chest. It was a pose that no matter his form Cosmos would always be able to recognise his warrior friend. He wiped his mouth with the back of his hand and stood a little straighter, he watched as Arcaeus' face broke out into a grin, one that felt contagious and had his own responding with a tilt of his lips.

"Feeling better?" His smug voice asked moments before he strode down the street. With a shake of his head he followed, his legs had started to become less shaky and his equilibrium had returned all be it slowly. His twin swords bounced against his back as he jogged to catch up with Arcaeus.

"So tell me, where and when are we, Arcaeus?"

Arcaeus stopped in front of a structure, the front made out of a clear substance and Cosmos reached out to touch it where Arcaeus' hand rested against it. This world was full of wonderful unusual things. He had seen glass before but only in small amounts and it was never this pure. He lifted his gaze to that of Arcaeus.

"I promise, Cosmos, I will tell you all soon, but first I have to see Arianna. I have to see for myself that she is ok." With that he tugged the entryway door open and stalked inside, Cosmos followed quickly and took in every detail as his mind attempted to adjust to this new strange world. A world so unbelievably different from his own. He followed Arcaeus as they started to climb the steps that would take them to a different level. Each step upwards reminded Cosmos that he had not long ago escaped from a mosaic and battled beasts from the underworld. His thighs burned as the climb continued flight after flight of stairs. The climb also brought back to mind that both he and Arcaeus were injured and he would need to see to their wounds at some point soon, he tried to ignore the burn of ripped flesh but he was starting to tire.

They climbed higher and higher, Cosmos peered over the railing and looked down, other than a brief jaunt up the side of the mountains near his home this was the highest he had ever been. Finally, Arcaeus stopped his climb and walked out onto a small landing with doors that were dotted here and there, he turned and faced Cosmos as he finished the climb.

"I thought you would prefer the stairs to the lift considering your reaction to the car."

Cosmos frowned, there was so much about this land, this time, that he didn't understand and it left him at a disadvantage and on edge.

"Don't make me regret saving your life, Arcaeus." His words held no heat as he caught his breath and stood to his full height then stalked towards his friend. "Now, you promised me food."

With a weary chuckle Arcaeus turned and walked towards a plain black door, the number 152 the only sign of its identity. 'Finally,' Cosmos thought, he would finally get some answers and, of course, food. But most importantly he was free.

A loud knock sounded at the door to Sonia's apartment, the noise filled the room and caused Arianna and Sonia to jump out of their skin. In silence they sat on the sofa and looked at each other, both gazes filled with fear.

"Arianna," Sonia whispered. "Do you think it's them?"

Arianna frowned and stayed silent.

"Do you think they have found us?"

They both jumped as the knock sounded again this time harder and louder than before. Arianna finally leant forward and whispered back.

"I don't think so, Sonnie, I don't think they would be polite enough to knock do you?"

In unison they peeked over the back of the sofa and eyed the corridor that led to the front door. Their eyes widened further as the knocking increased in its frequency. The hard bangs against the wooden door now caused the walls to vibrate with the force. Both Sonia and Arianna stayed frozen on the sofa, their hands gripped the back cushions, unable to look away. In one sudden movement the sound of cracking and splintering wood followed by a crash as the door was kicked off its hinges and sent flying into the corridor. Pictures that were hung fell to the floor and dust and splinters flew as growls and shouts echoed into the room.

"Arianna, where the fuck are you?" The deep growl reached both Arianna and Sonia and caused a high pitch squeal to erupt from Arianna before she bolted over the back of the sofa and ran towards the hall. Sonia watched as Arcaeus appeared from the corridor and without breaking his stride he swept Arianna up and into his arms, their mouths met in a flurry of kisses and arms wrapped tight around each other. Their love and relief at being together again was almost palpable.

Sonia sagged on the sofa and rested her forehead against the back cushions. Thank god he made it. She was filled with a sense of relief. She felt like an interloper as their exchange of words reached her.

"Oh, Arcaeus, you are ok? What happened? Are you hurt?" These words flew out in between kisses and Arcaeus' replies were just as sporadic.

"Fuck, Anya, baby, did they hurt you? Let me check you are ok. No, wait, don't move yet let me hold you a bit longer."

A smile played at Sonia's lips and she lifted her head a little so she could peek at the couple, her mouth opened to yell, "get a room," but her mouth froze and only a squeak escaped as a large, slightly familiar, male stormed past the couple and into the room.

"Oh for the love of Aphrodite put each other down. Arcaeus you promised me food and I see none."

Sonia heard Arianna giggle a little but her entire focus was now on the male that dominated the centre of the room. Huge muscles, biceps flexed as they crossed over an equally muscled chest. The hilt of two swords could be seen behind him. His face a combination of hard lines and soft contours, a contradiction in itself but somehow worked. Smouldering eyes that had now locked onto her own. Emotions flickered in their depths as his deep gravelly voice pulled Sonia out of her perusal.

"You!" The male stalked over to her hiding place. "You are the one that freed me."

Sonia scrambled back onto the sofa.

"Huh? What? I don't know what you are talking about. I don't even know who the hell you are." She fired back with more bravado then she felt inside, she now lay back on bent elbows. She attempted to sit up but the male leant over the sofa, his eyes full of anger.

"You, it is your fault these creatures have been freed, what in the name of Zeus were you thinking? You meddle in things you know nothing of, you silly woman."

"WHAT!?" Sonia, forgetting how close he loomed over her, scrambled to her knees, her injured hand forgotten as she pointed a finger at the male. "Back off you overgrown Neanderthal. It was not my fault and don't you dare talk to me like that you… you turd." Her finger almost jabbed the male in his hard chest before his large callused hand wrapped around her own. She gasped as a feeling similar to that of an electric shock coursed through her and hit her with her second vision of the day.

Her breaths were more like pants and they came out fast as she looked from the pale cream ceiling of her room to the golden head that now looked up at her from between her legs. His eyes smouldered with pure and unadulterated lust. In a slow deliberate movement, he licked his lips, his voice a rasp of words that vibrated against her core.

"You taste like ambrosia, my little Hellcat, so damn good I could feast on you

all day long." He bent his head again and took her clit between his lips and sucked hard. Sonia's back bowed and a moan escaped her lips as he pushed a thick digit into her wet core and twisted. She felt herself clench hard around his finger as he bit down on her clit. Her body erupting into an almost instant orgasm.

Sonia blinked as she drew in a deep breath. The angry words of the male penetrated her mind and brought her fully out of the vision.

"Woman, did you not hear me, is your mind addled?"

"What? Did you not see that?" Sonia mumbled and tried to tug her hand away from the male, her body was still in a state of pure euphoria from the vision and her heart rate had yet to settle back to a normal rhythm.

"Woman, I said how did you injure yourself, and why have you not seen a healer and have it tended to?"

Sonia looked up at the male, her head spun from the combination of blood loss and the intensity of the vision. A headache that had never really gone began to pound behind her eyes. She focused on the huge male in front of her and dragged her hand away. With shaky legs she climbed off the sofa.

"You, you arse! Don't you touch me and don't talk to me for that matter. I don't know who the hell you are and quite frankly I don't want to know so just back the hell off and get away from me." Sonia took two steps and walked past the male, he reached out and grasped her arm, in an attempt to stop her. She looked up into his face and through gritted teeth she grated out, "I said don't touch…"

Her eyes rolled to the back of her head as her mind went blank and her body collapsed into the arms of the male.

Chapter Eleven

It was a good job Cosmos was a skilled warrior as well as having better than average reactions; if he hadn't been quick he would have missed the female as she lost consciousness. In one swift movement Cosmos swept the female into his arms and he couldn't help but take a deep breath of her scent. The alluring fragrance reminded him of home but also of the frustration of his imprisonment. As much as he fought it he could feel his body start to respond, and it responded quickly. This female was dangerous, somehow she had freed both himself and the creatures from the mosaic but what he was still unsure of was how and if she could do it again. The prospect of more of those things set loose upon the mortal world was a nightmare straight from Tartarus itself. Cosmos looked to Arcaeus in his unusual form and then to Arianna who looked much the same except for her strange clothing.

"Where should I place her? I will have need of medicines for her injured hand."

Arianna said nothing, but her face reflected the worry she so obviously felt for her friend. She lifted her hand and pointed towards the closed door that was opposite the entrance to the room where he was currently situated. With ease he adjusted his grip slightly on the red head and stepped towards the directed room. He was eager if not impatient to set the female down and had had to force back a growl of annoyance as he waited for Arianna to open the door. Almost immediately he shouldered his way into the room and stalked towards the bed. He was surprised by its size, it nearly took up the full room. With a gentleness he wasn't aware he possessed he laid her down upon the soft bedding. He watched almost fascinated as she instantly curled into a ball on her right side, her brow puckered as if she was in pain. Before he could stop himself he reached out and brushed a long lock of hair away from her face. The sense of touch was overwhelming; her skin was as soft as silk. When he had been trapped inside the mosaic all he had been left with smell. Everything else had moved so slowly that his other senses were unable to engage fully. Now he was free he was more than eager to experience everything being mortal had to offer.

He wouldn't admit to anyone but himself that when he had grasped the female's hand, they connected. He had seen her vision, seen it and was now unable to get the image of how she looked as she had climaxed out of his mind. He could still remember how she had tasted as if her essence still coated his lips, if he closed his eyes he was able to recollect how her core had felt as it had clenched down on his finger as he had fucked her with it. His body had reacted instantly and was even now still hard from just the mere thought of the vision they had shared.

No, he couldn't allow this, he couldn't allow this woman to distract him. The fact she was having visions as well as being the one that had freed the creatures meant that she was special, special and dangerous. Her beauty in itself was a distraction, and it was something Cosmos was determined to ignore. Yes, he was drawn to her beauty and he had actually enjoyed it when she had stuck out her chin and attempted to shout him down. He had always enjoyed women with a little fire. His mission now was simple — as well as hunting down the remaining creatures and sending them back to Hades, he now had to find out more about this female and then decide if he should destroy her for the sake of this modern mortal world. If she was the key and was capable of unleashing those beasts upon the world then he would do his duty. He watched the rise and fall of her chest and felt an unfamiliar tug in his own, she looked so vulnerable as she lay curled up, a part of him ached to curl up next to her, wrap his arms around her waist and tug her into the warmth of his body.

With a growl he knelt next to the bed and took her injured hand into his own, he forced the feelings of affection and comfort aside. He didn't want nor need them. With gentle fingers he peeled back the sodden bandage away from the flesh. Blood welled from the deep laceration that bisected her palm. Cosmos, unable to hold back, winced as the blood continued to pour from her palm. This was the evidence that proved she was how they had been freed. Cosmos closed his eyes and took a deep breath and pulled at his special gift. A gift he had never told anyone about. He relaxed his shoulders and opened his eyes. Colours swirled around the flesh of the female's hand, her aura bright and innocent. Yet there in the centre of her palm black and greys oozed from the wound, fingers of magic that were deep ingrained into the palm. Only magic, magic of the gods, could have caused a wound this nasty and that wouldn't stop bleeding. Cosmos frowned; if the gods were involved then he would have to work quickly, and that also meant the decision of whether or not to kill the female had been made for him. A knock at the door brought Cosmos out of his thoughts, he looked up to see Arianna walk into the room with her arms full of fresh bandages and other supplies he didn't recognise. With a tentative smile she placed them on the bed then gasped as she looked past Cosmos and to the wound on the hand of the female.

"Oh my god, she told me she had only scratched her palm. We should really take her to the hospital and get that seen to." Before Arianna had a chance to try and wake the female he grabbed her hand.

"No leave her be, Arianna," he tried to gentle his voice. "This I can deal with. I assure you I have spent many a time patching Arcaeus up, he can attest to my skills." He released Arianna's hand and set to work to dress the wound. He grabbed the packs of white material, unsure of what they were but he assumed they could be used to pack the wound. He held it against the palm and looked up to see Arianna, she watched him closely.

"I do not know how she did this, but I believe it is why the creatures and I are here now and not locked inside that mosaic." Cosmos stood and stretched his back then tucked the now freshly bandaged hand next to the female before he took hold of a blanket and draped it over her. He may need to kill her but it didn't mean he wouldn't be nice to her from now on. He had to admit he had been a bit of an ass, as Arianna would say.

"Arianna, don't worry for your friend, as you can see she is now resting. Please show me to a cleansing room for I still have the stench of the underworld clinging to me. Then you can inform Arcaeus he promised me food. I must warn you, I am starving." Cosmos smiled and moved to leave the room but his steps halted as Arianna stood and stared down at the female.

"Will she be ok, Cosmos?"

He placed his hand on her shoulder and nodded, "Yes, Arianna, your friend will be ok."

"Sonia," Arianna responded as she finally moved to walk past Cosmos, she tilted her head up to look up at him. "Her name is Sonia, Cosmos, and she is my family."

Cosmos watched Arianna as she left the room with one final look at the sleeping female.

"Sonia," he smiled. The name suited her.

"Sonia."

Chapter Twelve

Memories swirled as Sonia sunk in and out of consciousness. Memories of when she was a child and her parents used to tell fantastical stories of the gods of old, memories mixed with dreams and fantasies that melded together and created a world unlike any other. Sonia dreamt of a handsome warrior battling creatures born of nightmares; he openly defied the gods and took pleasure in thwarting their control. Passion and sacrifice bloomed, it gave her a feeling of love and belonging. A blonde with hair the length of the fairy tale princess Rapunzel but the colour of spun gold, almost as if the sun itself, had kissed her head, entrusting this female with its precious rays, her eyes so laden with emotion it captured Sonia's own and trapped her in a torrent of feeling. The voice so angelic filtered into Sonia's awareness.

"Sonia, trust the warrior for he is the only male able to help you and protect you even from yourself. Be at peace and trust in love, Oracle, and let fate takes its destined course."

Her words faded as the dream changed to reality, her form vanished after a blink of Sonia's eyes as she focused now on the wood of her bedside table and the blinking red lights of her alarm clock. Sonia remained in the same position, curled on her side with both hands tucked under the pillow as she let the thoughts of the dream filter through her mind as well as memories of the previous events.

She winced as the full pain from her hand hit her hard, her body folded in on itself into a tighter ball as she breathed through the shooting pains that radiated from her palm and up her arm. Once the pain had lessened somewhat she rolled over and into a seated position, her legs dangled off the side.

"Ugh, that's just nasty," Sonia smacked her lips together, her mouth felt like it was full of cotton roll, and the constant headache had again taken up home behind her eyes. She was getting fed up of the headaches now and they always seemed to get worse after she had had one of the strange visions. Even her dreams were becoming deranged.

Sonia looked down at her heavily bandaged hand, she turned it over so her palm was faced up and noticed that the dressings had been changed but as before she could already see fresh blood had started to seep through the gauze. On slightly shaky legs Sonia got to her feet, she stood slowly and approached her dressing table, she grabbed a pack of facial wipes from the top and looked at her reflection. Her hair was a complete mess and resembled the back end of a horse, only her pony tail wasn't as pretty. Dark circles underlined Sonia's eyes and made her look like she hadn't just been in the world of nod. Her face on a whole was pale, well, paler than usual and it made the red of her hair look even brighter. Her only feature that didn't look exhausted were her eyes, they seemed to shimmer almost as if they were full of tears but they remained dry as a bone. Sonia pulled at the small tie that held some of her long hair up and tugged and freed her locks, she winced as she again knocked her hand and issued a few choice words. After a few deep breaths she took hold of her hairbrush and started to attempt to tame her hair, the knots and snags caught and fought against the brush.

"Ouch… Dammit that hurts… Stupid bloody hair, one of these days I'm going to chop you all off I bloody swear it." Her tirade disturbed by a soft knock at the door, the door opened almost immediately and Arianna's concerned face appeared in the gap.

"Sonnie, are you ok? How are you feeling?"

Sonia forced a smile and nodded to her friend and turned back to the mirror as she continued to fight with her hair, she tried to keep her voice as cheery as possible.

"I'm ok, Anya, I'm sorry for scaring you. I think everything that had happened just got to me." Sonia placed the brush onto the table and smiled at her friend in the mirror as she took a facial wipe and proceeded to clean her face. "Did I miss anything?"

Arianna smiled and walked into the room, she lifted her leg and perched on the end of the bed and watched as Sonia made herself feel a little more human.

"Not much to be honest, Sonnie. You've been out for about four hours and the 'boys' have been playing catch up."

Sonia stilled then threw the used wipe into the waste basket by the table and then took a hold of her moisturiser.

"Catching up? Are you telling me you know the 'Troy extra'?"

Arianna laughed and nodded.

"Troy extra? Really, Sonnie, wrong era." Arianna grinned and leant over the bed and grabbed a pillow then hugged it to her chest as she crossed her legs and she moved further onto the bed.

"Cosmos, aka Troy extra, was Arcaeus' second in command back in Ancient Greece. From what I've heard, well, when I concentrated, they were very close and have known each other since childhood."

Sonia turned and leant back against the dressing table and listened, she wanted to know more about this warrior even if their first meeting hadn't been of the friendly kind. Something about him pulled at her and intrigued her into learning all she could about the warrior that was stone.

"Cosmos is still trying to get used to Arcaeus looking completely different to how he used to look. But once a warrior always a warrior, I guess," Arianna shrugged and then smiled. "They have been showing off their injuries as well, as if they somehow make them manlier."

Sonia rolled her eyes and smiled back at her friend, she still felt very unsure about the new warrior Cosmos, as much as a part of her welcomed the fact he wasn't just a painting. From the moment they had set eyes on each other there had been an immediate intense atmosphere. He seemed aggressive and domineering as well as showing his obvious dislike towards her and blame for the events that had happened. Sonia pushed away from the table and started towards the door.

"Come on then, let's go and see what they are up to now."

Arianna practically bounced off the bed and sped out of the room, clearly eager to be with her man even though they seemed inseparable. The moment Sonia's bedroom door had opened they were both assaulted by the delicious smell of pizza as it filled the apartment. Sonia's stomach growled loudly, it reminded Sonia that she hadn't eaten since breakfast and due to the attack in the park they had all completely missed lunch and now due to her hitting the deck she had almost missed out on tea. Yeah, it had been a while since she had eaten and a hungry Sonia was a hangry Sonia. With an inner chuckle she followed Arianna into the lounge, as if on their own accord her eyes zeroed in on Cosmos and this time she let herself explore more than just his face. Of course she had that memorised right down to the small scar that bisected his left eyebrow and disappeared into his hairline. It wasn't her fault he had been serious eye candy when he had been in the mosaic. But now he was larger than life and, in short, a hell of a lot more intimidating. Even as he reclined on the sofa and stuffed pizza into his mouth like a dying man. He had an aura of danger and even his obvious relaxed position seemed false, almost like he was waiting to spring into action and kill something. Sonia chuckled to herself as she imagined He-Man from the cartoons battling monsters. Turned out she had her very own camped out on her sofa.

As Sonia walked into the lounge she watched as Cosmos flicked her a disinterested gaze before he resumed his assault on the pizza box. From the looks of things both he and Arcaeus had already polished off two extra-large pizzas from Dominoes and they were now on their third. Without a word Sonia headed into the kitchen to grab a drink, that funky taste just wouldn't leave and she could murder a glass of wine. She pulled two glasses from the shelf and grabbed the bottle of chardonnay from the fridge before she straightened her shoulders and walked back into the lounge. A quick scan made her realise the only place left to sit was next to Cosmos. So after she had handed Arianna her glass she filled her own and then curled up on the end of the sofa and avoided any eye contact with the warrior. She wanted to avoid all contact because she definitely didn't want a repeat of what had happened earlier.

With her wine in one hand and a stolen slice of margarita in the other she settled back and listened to the males talk. The girls' presence already forgotten as they remembered tales of old. Sonia's only evidence that Cosmos had noticed her was a stiffening of his posture and the clench of his fists.

"Oh, well, not my fault he's a complete tool," Sonia thought. If he had a problem then that was his deal, she only hoped he would get over his issues soon, especially if they had to work together for much longer.

Chapter Thirteen

Apollo watched the mortal, Archie, as he paced across the lab that held the mosaic, the short balding man was giving off a healthy dose of fear as he attempted to answer the god's questions. He knew that Apollo wasn't happy but the mortal had no idea why. Apollo stood and folded his huge arms across his chest. He really had to try and control his temper. He had already lost a few servants because of it.

"Mortal, I repeat. Where is the girl? You said she would be here and she has only been able to release a handful of my creatures. This as you well know is not what I wanted." Apollo moved towards the curator, his temper rising with each step "And, Archie," he said with a sneer. "You also know I ALWAYS get what I want."

As the god of the sun approached the cowering form of the curator he ran his fingertips over the surface of the mosaic, the sounds of the mortal's distress gave him the sense of power and control that he constantly craved. His form pulsed with power, even leashed as it was it filled the room and caused more whimpering from the curator. As soon as the god's fingertips traced the stonework it rippled as if a pebble had been thrown onto the surface of a pond or lake. Almost immediately the picture depicted changed and morphed into a nightmare. Gone were the fallen bodies of the creatures that had been killed by the warrior, their forms hidden by rows upon rows of creatures awaiting release. Fangs extended as well as claws; they merely awaited Apollo's order.

"Soon, my pets, soon," Apollo grinned and pulled his hand back. An idea had formed in his head but first he wanted another question answering. "Mortal, come, do not fear me, you have done well." Apollo waited as the curator got to his feet and approached slowly, the god continued on. "Archie, pray tell me where is the warrior that was also in the mosaic?"

The mortal's face snapped up and then looked at the mosaic, his fingers frantically searched the surface for any sign of the warrior. With an obvious desperation he shook his head as he slowly realised the warrior was no longer present. Apollo grinned. Yes, they had had a set back with the girl vanishing before she could free all of his creatures but the portal remained open which meant her wound also remained open and that she was still close by. The god's grin turned feral as his idea started to click into place. His magic that was reinforced and made stronger as he had tapped into Aphrodite's powers was working and would mean the girl would bleed out before the wound would close. But he would rather bleed her out himself than wait for it to happen slowly. He had to push this along faster and what way to call to the girl than to use her favourite curator.

As the curator was leant down over the mosaic Apollo approached behind, the malicious glint in his eyes hidden, so entranced in his search he was unaware that his fate had already been decided. Apollo's right hand gripped the mortal's shoulder, a golden knife held in his left as he sent Archibald to the underworld. Apollo stepped back as the body of the mortal slumped over the mosaic, it set off the ripples but his form never broke the surface. His life's blood poured from the deep laceration to his neck, the cut almost severing the head. The death stroke itself had been quick and clean, as a blessing from the god himself it had been instantaneous. Apollo watched as the blood ran across the stone surface, the surface pulsed and slowly absorbed the red fluid. Before the ripples had ended Apollo pushed the body of the curator into the mosaic. He beamed an almost smug smile as the body vanished and was accepted into the depths, only to appear as a depiction — his body now lay under the feet of the waiting hoard.

The surface rippled again and slowly a creature emerged from the stone, his claws scraped against the stone and created deep grooves, clear evidence of the damage that they were capable of doing. Once his long body was free he stepped down onto the floor and faced the god. Saliva bubbled from the corner of its mouth, its feral eyes skittered all around, never focusing on one spot.

Apollo's plan was working, although the curator's blood wasn't strong enough to finish the job the oracle had started it had allowed one of the creatures to pass through. His death and blood was payment for its passage. Now he just had to steal some more of his sister's magic and tweak a few things and he had the perfect way to lure the oracle back.

"You want to free your brethren?" Apollo approached the creature, its nod almost missed. "Good, I have need of you."

The golden god continued on and circled the creature, his excitement grew.

"I need the girl and you will be the one to fetch her for me, is that understood?" Again the creature bobbed his head in agreement as it gave off feral growls and the occasional hiss. Apollo stopped in front of the creature and grabbed it by the chin, tilting its red feral eyes to meet his own turquoise blue ones.

"I need her alive and unharmed…for now. Is that understood?"

The creature blinked his answer and Apollo released its chin and turned to wipe his hand on a cloth that had been left on the worktop. His commanding voice filled the room.

"Bring her to me and I shall release the rest of your brethren on this mortal world." The god of the sun smiled again and waved his hand towards the salivating monster, a ripple of flesh and a pulse of bright golden light erupted and then left. The form of the creature gone and replaced by a carbon copy of the curator. The only tell-tale difference were the eyes: blood red now replaced deep brown.

"Use this form to gain her trust and bring her back to this room. You have two days." The god turned his back on the creature and stalked back towards the mosaic. "GO! NOW!"

The creature bolted out of the lab, Apollo's only hope was that it didn't go feral before it got to the girl, now he had something else to worry about. The warrior that had been trapped with his creatures was also free — this he couldn't have — he either needed to die or he needed to be returned back to the mosaic. Apollo would prefer the latter, there was just something about a slow painful death that made him all tingly and happy. He remembered this warrior briefly from when he'd had Arcaeus tied up, he had escorted that female, and if memory served him right he was Arcaeus'right hand man, With that in mind Apollo needed a plan to trap the warrior, irt also brought to his attention that Arcaeus now had backup and it was no doubt the pair of them that had dispatched some of the creatures that had escaped. The god grumbled before he snapped his fingers and vanished in a flash of golden light. He had work to do.

Chapter Fourteen

Soft snores woke Cosmos from his light doze; he was still sprawled on the large sofa, his arms stretched across the back and his head was tilted backwards. He blinked a few times to remove the remanence of sleep and slowly got his bearings. His eyes scanned the room not missing one detail. From his sprawled position he could see Arcaeus was sat on the opposite sofa, his friend's eyes entirely focused on Arianna who lay curled up in his lap. Cosmos was surprised by the tenderness his friend openly displayed. Back in his own time men never showed affection or emotion of any kind, it was viewed as a weakness and there had been times both Arcaeus and himself had seen the end of a lash for showing even the slightest sign. But as he watched the warrior, every touch, every look openly showed the love he felt for Arianna. Cosmos had never in his life wanted those things, he had been content enough to fight whenever he was called and if he needed relief, it wasn't hard to find a willing woman with an open bed. As a fighter he was well sort after as the ladies wanted a beast between their legs. Arcaeus had on occasion had to help him out of some dicey situations with angry husbands. Cosmos repressed the smirk that wanted to break out as he let the memories fly through his mind. He released a long quiet sigh, before the incident, before he had become trapped inside of that mosaic, a small, tiny part of him yearned for what Arcaeus had with Arianna. When he had watched them interact back home he had seen them fall for each other and knowing he may never experience that he had wanted it more.

Cosmos felt like an intruder as he again watched his friend slowly wake Arianna, privacy was already hard in such a large room, so he did what he could and focused his gaze on the cause for his recent position and current confusion. Sonia's soft snores again gained his attention, they called out to him and made him want to gather her sleeping form into his arms and hold her close.

"Where in Zeus' thunderbolt did that come from? I don't even like her and she sure as hell don't like me," he quietly mumbled as he looked over at her. He would admit that there was something appealing about her, he wouldn't and really couldn't deny that she was beautiful, but the minute she opened that smart mouth, well, that just put him off. He hadn't even known or spoken to her much but that coupled with the fact she was the cause for arrival of the creatures he was better to just steer clear.

He didn't take a lot to realise with her death the creatures would be returned back into the mosaic, but that being said so would he. He knew and would bet the ambrosia on Olympus that his future was about as long as hers. What he didn't want was to be sucked back into that mosaic and he would destroy it first or die trying. He had to have a plan and finding out who was behind all of this was the start. As Cosmos' thoughts wandered this way and that he continued to watch Sonia. She was curled on her side and faced him, her hands like when he had put her to bed were tucked under her cheek. Her face was relaxed and only a flicker of a frown marred her features, her eyelids fluttered as she dreamt. Her continued snores so ladylike caused a smile to crease his mouth. A quiet cough drew his attention away for Sonia and onto that of Arcaeus who had been watching him just as closely as he had watched Sonia. His friend's voice was calm and quiet as he tried not to disturb the females.

"I am going to take Arianna home. I've already called a taxi," Arcaeus grinned and held up the item he called a phone. "This Uber-app is the dogs," he smirked as Cosmos paled at the mere thought of the metal beast they had ridden inside of. He nodded in response

"I will be in touch tomorrow. If you have need of anything get Sonia to contact Arianna."

In one smooth movement Arcaeus stood with Arianna still sleeping in his arms, another nod in Cosmos direction and Arcaeus headed out of the room, he stopped just short of the door frame and turned his head to look at Cosmos, his voice quiet but serious.

"Look after Sonia, Cosmos. She is family to Arianna and my girl would not appreciate any harm befalling her."

Cosmos opened his mouth to answer but Arcaeus had already left, the front door barely made a sound as the newly repaired wood closed. It left him alone with his thoughts and the sleeping Sonia. He needed a plan now more than ever and he needed one that wouldn't annoy Arcaeus as well as sending those creatures back to the underworld. Cosmos closed his eyes and leant his head back against the back of the sofa. He would start his master plan by getting some more rest, coming out of purgatory was, in short, exhausting.

Chapter Fifteen

"Aphrodite! Why have you summoned me away from the underworld?" Hades' voice boomed throughout the temple dedicated to love. He was unable to stop the sneer that crossed his face as he looked over the paintings that depicted love in all its forms and a hell of a lot of sex. Hades strolled further into the room and his eyes roamed this way and that before he faced one wall where a graphic image had been painted, he tilted his head to the right and his eyes widened as he stepped forward.

"Surely that's not even…" His head tilted the other way as he then took a step back. "Wow, I guess that is possible."

With a manly snort Hades continued on into the domain of love herself, he flexed his fingers and rolled his neck. He was irritated, he never ventured out of the underworld unless for something important and he didn't get invited out much, but that was beside the point. He was irritated that he was currently being ignored and she had failed to answer him.

"Goddess, I am in no moods to play your games!"

Nothing. Not even the whisper of footsteps — strange. Aphrodite was what Hades classed as an annoyingly affectionate goddess. It was known throughout all of Olympus that she always made a visitor to her temple welcome so to be ignored when she had summoned him seemed very odd. A flutter of wings alerted Hades to the presence of Aphrodite's companion. Only a few of his fellow immortals took the time and had companions, most were far too selfish and full of their own self-importance to spend some of their own immortality on another being. For Aphrodite to do so showed she truly was love incarnate.

"My lord, Hades, thank you for answering my goddess's call. Please let me go fetch her for you. She is probably unawares of your arrival" Metons voiced cracked as he attempted to calm his panting,the journey from the underworld not a quick one without the immortal's powers to aid them.

Hades held up his hand to halt the Eagle.

"Hold, Meton." The god of the underworld waited for the great eagle to catch his breath. "I have already called for your goddess twice, why does she not answer?"

The golden bird visibly paled, concern marred his feathered features as he took flight and flew further into the inner sanctum of the temple. A loud gasp followed by a frantic cry for help from Meton had Hades moving towards the eagle's voice.

"Oh no, my lady! Lord Hades, please hurry she needs assistance."

On swift feet the god moved further into the temple and entered the main chamber. In the centre of the room stood a large dais, the throne like chair carved with more images of frolicking naked mortals, gods and other strange beings. Cushions were scattered all around the room showing the goddess preferred her patrons to be comfortable when they visited. Upon the raised platform before the chair lay the still form of the goddess, her face was pale and no longer held the natural glow of power that the immortals usually held. Her breathing was shallow and came in short sharp gasps.

Hades bent down next to Aphrodite and placed his hand upon her head as he looked up at Meton. "Tell me, what is wrong with her?"

The great eagle shook his head as he gazed down at the goddess. "I do not know, my lord. She mentioned that she did not feel well just before I left to fetch you." The golden bird sighed then looked up at the god. "Can immortals fall ill?"

Hades brushed Aphrodite's hair away from her face, her skin was cold to the touch and clammy and with ease he gathered the goddess into his arms and stood.

"No, we don't fall ill, Meton. This in itself is highly unusual. Show me to her chamber and let us get her settled in comfort and then discuss a plan and decide whether to make my brother aware of the situation. This is worrying indeed."

Meton bowed his feathered head. His eyes showed all of his worry and concern he felt for his goddess, with a nod he turned and took flight.

"This way, my lord, Hades."

Hades' footsteps filled the silence as he followed the eagle, his thoughts filled with concern for his brethren but also worry for all immortals. If someone had discovered how to kill them then they would all be at risk. The thought of having to accompany one of his own into the fields of Elyssia was unheard of and if truth be told it would be painful. They were created to live forever, watching over the mortal world. The mortals would tear the world apart if left unchecked. His own mortality wasn't something that crossed his mind and he took it for granted that he was forever living. Maybe now he would see it in a different light, especially when he had yet to experience something that the mortals themselves took for granted. Love. It felt ironic he was now here to assist love herself and a small part of him hoped he could use that in his favour. He did after all hold one of Aphrodite's love potions, he was just clueless on how to use it.

As he entered Aphrodite's bedchamber he was taken back by how classy it looked. He had expected more frolicking naked forms and depictions of sex, but surprisingly there were none. The marble walls were kept pristine and free from paintings and mosaics, other than one. This one covered the entire wall and simply showed the sunset over the ocean. The ripple of the waves almost real as they lapped at the sands. White clothes lined with pink surrounded another raised platform, this housed a large circular mattress covered with pink and white pillows. A small fountain lay just beyond, the lyrical sound of the water was the only other sound in the room.

Hades quickly approached the bed and laid the goddess down gently upon the mattress and covered her with a blanket in an attempt to ward off the chill. Her form huddled under the cover as she visibly shivered. He then turned and faced the golden eagle, his voice firm but kind.

"Now, Meton, tell me all and swiftly."

The eagle looked at his goddess as she lay on her bed, her eyes had sunken like in sand and she looked pale and grey. He had no choice but to put his trust in the hands of the god of the underworld. He would start at the beginning, the very beginning with Arianna and Arcaeus' story.

Meton, the sole companion of Aphrodite goddess of love, launched into his tale of how the goddess had become involved in the lives of both mortals and in turn started the fight against Apollo. Meton continued on, he talked about the atrocious deeds Apollo had done including the torture of Arcaeus and his treatment of Arianna in both her lives. Meton then explained about the more recent events that involved Sonia and the warrior, Cosmos, as well as the evolvement of the mosaic. He watched as Hades started to pace across the chamber. The eagle's words churned around and around in his mind. Finally, he turned back to the eagle as he watched over his goddess.

"Meton, I believe I can help, but in return you must promise yours and Aphrodite's assistance when I have need of it."

"Anything, my lord. Anything if it saves my goddess's life," the eagle blurted out, the desperation obvious in his voice. With an answering nod Hades called out, the power he held flexed from his hand and in a flash of purple light an intricately carved silver bowl stood before him. It was placed on a stunningly beautiful stand also from silver that was carved to show the souls reaching for Elyssia. He placed his large palm over the surface of the pool and called out, the power in his voice crackled in the air.

"Show me the mosaic, show me the warrior."

The surface instantly rippled before it changed, the silver liquid transformed into a window. It showed the lab that housed the mosaic, the stonework's image now completely filled with creatures as they waited to be freed. Within a blink of an eye the image changed again. This time it showed a comfy room and there, lounged upon a sofa, the warrior sat, his head tilted back in sleep and next to him curled up into a ball lay the red head known as Sonia. Hades raised an eyebrow as he changed his sight and glimpsed upon the mortal's aura, hers was almost bright white, a tell-tale sign of an oracle, but lined around the edges like ink that seeped onto white paper was blackness that tinged her very soul. The only explanation was the wound she had gained from the mosaic. Dark magic indeed and one that would need care to extinguish. The god's gaze moved again towards the warrior, he remembered watching this mortal as he battled alongside Arcaeus on the fields of punishment. Even now in sleep he looked lethal, his body honed into a weapon. But something wasn't right, his aura was completely different. Hades leant forward in hopes of understanding more, his voice full of disbelief.

"Well bugger me."

Meton raised his head and looked at the god, shock etched across his features before he moaned.

"My lord, not you as well."

Hades faced the bird and just grinned. It turned out Aphrodite wasn't the only immortal who had started picking up mortal sayings.

Chapter Sixteen

Cosmos had drifted to sleep, this he knew just as he knew the temple he now stood in no longer existed and was a figment of his deepest thoughts and dreams. Even knowing this he enjoyed the feelings that coursed through him, it had been a long time since he had felt this relaxed and at peace. He took deep breaths of the clear, clean air and let himself smile. Although this was a dream he would enjoy every second and relish the contentment that coursed through him.

"Cosmos?" The soft feminine voice called out to Cosmos from across the temple, her voice one he had not heard from in a very long time yet one he would never ever forget.

"Mother?" His own voice laced with curiosity and he watched as she almost floated across the marble towards him. Her hair was still the golden colour of the sun and her eyes sparkled like gems. She looked just as beautiful as the last day he had seen her alive.

In a delicate move she took his large callused hands into her own. "My darling boy," she brought his hands, specifically his knuckles, to her lips and placed a kiss upon them.

"Look at the fine handsome warrior you have become." Her smile instantly filled a void inside Cosmos' heart, deep down he knew this feeling would never last but he embraced it all the same. He looked down into eyes that held such warmth.

"Oh, Mother, I have missed you. I have missed your wisdom." She smiled sadly up at him and lifted her hand and cupped his cheek, the heat from her palm almost real.

"I know, my darling. I have missed you also but you cannot linger here. Your fate has already been written and the task ahead will test your courage, strength and honour." Her eyes filled with tears as she moved her hand from his cheek and placed it upon his chest over his heart. "My dear boy, this task will test you more than you have been tested in your life." She stepped back and severed their connection.

"I just pray you will forgive me when your trials are over but please never forget, my son, that I love you. Never doubt it."

Cosmos placed his hand over his heart right where her hand had been and bowed. His words also laced with sadness as he knew without a doubt he wouldn't see his mother again, not until he himself entered the fields of Elyssia.

"I will never forget, Momma." His use of his childhood name for her caused her to smile, she raised her fingers to her lips.

"Trust your instincts, my son," her voice now a mere whisper as her form faded into light. "Love her, Cosmos."

Aphrodite opened her eyes slowly and took in her surroundings. She recognised the pristine white marble of her chamber walls, this alone managed to relax her. All she could remember was walking towards her dais to prepare for the arrival of Hades when blackness had descended. Before she had totally succumbed to the lack void she was certain she had heard Apollo's irritating voice, she had no doubt her current affliction stemmed from his misdeeds. Never in her long existence had she felt this weak and powerless, the closest she had ever been was after a night with some of the other goddess's during a ritual. She winced as she remembered them stealing a bottle of Dionysus' most potent wine. All of them had spent the next day in their chambers feeling like they had been knocked about by a Minotaur as well as unable to stomach anything.

Aphrodite tried to roll over. She was unable to stop the moan that escaped her lips as her body protested, every muscle ached, her head throbbed and her throat was so dry she felt she had gargled with sand.

"My lady, how do you feel?" Metons calm and soothing voice pulled her gaze to where her companion was perched, a chair had been placed by the side of her bed on the raised platform. His open look of concern and worry pulled at her heart. Her voice a quiet croak as she tried to answer; her smile hoping to allay some of his fears.

"Meton… a drink. Please."

She watched as her feathered friend lifted his head and looked past her, a deep gravelly voice pulled her attention to her right and Aphrodite was unable to hide the shock that flashed across her face. Large gentle hands helped her turn over and then lift her into a sitting position. Hades then helped arrange the pillows behind her so she could sit comfortably before he picked up a goblet that resided on a small table next to her bed. Her eyes watched as he held the goblet to her lips and urged her to drink the fresh spring water. After her first tentative sip she took more in a hope to dispel the disgusting taste that had taken residence in her throat. Once she had had her fill Aphrodite turned her face and pulled away, using the pads of her fingers to wipe away the moisture at the corner of her mouth. Her voice still croaky she nodded at Hades.

"Thank you."

Hades placed the goblet back onto the table and turned to look down at the goddess, his face revealed nothing of what was currently going through his mind. Hades, as with all of the male gods, was gorgeous with long straight hair that fell well past his broad shoulders, its colour so black it held a bluish tinge to it when sunlight or moonlight hit; his face was all sharp angles and defined the term masculinity; the only softness came from his lips, perfectly shaped, full and just begged to be touched and kissed. It was his eyes that captured though, a stunning royal blue with flecks of silver. Perfect copies of the sky that covered the realm of the underworld. They held an inner glow that left any doubt that he was anything but an immortal. Unlike the other gods he was double the size and as one of the three top dogs he had power and it showed. Muscles that bulged with every movement and flexed with every breath. If Aphrodite had been mortal, he would only have to smile and she would have been happy to perform any of the paintings that covered her temple walls. Luckily she was immune and definitely didn't look at the god in that way. She shuddered slightly, he was basically her uncle and that was just plain freaky regardless of what the so called history books said about their doings on Olympus.

Unlike his brothers Hades held none of the arrogance and he always tended to hold himself back, there always seemed to be a sadness that surrounded him and she didn't think it came from his charges in the underworld. It was rare for the god to leave his home deep in the bowels of the earth, so for him to be here at this moment was a rare gift indeed and one that she wouldn't squander. Her mouth opened again to say her thanks but his next words stopped her short.

"Why are those mortals so important to you?" He now stood at the end of her bed, his huge frame almost seemed to grow larger, then he turned to pace. "What do you gain by helping them? It is well known we hold little if no power in the modern world. The mortals in that time no longer seek to worship us, they don't even believe in us anymore… So why?"

He stopped his pacing and folded his well-muscled arms across his equally large chest and just looked at her, his face this time revealed a look of pure confusion.

"I do not understand goddess, why do you need to be involved?"

Aphrodite tilted her head as she prepared her answer, she had to be careful with how she dealt with this god and she had to choose her words wisely if she wanted his help. But his words had struck something within her. How long had it been since he had left his sanctuary in the underworld and taken the effort to actually watch the mortals both of the ancient world and this modern one.

"Why not?" Her voice answered quietly, his answering frown urged her on. "Why shouldn't I help? When was the last time you took notice of the cares of the living instead of the dead? Regardless of the time they live in the mortals deserve a little help from love. The world has been so full of war and destruction as well as the creation of modern technology that the happier things in life have been forgotten." Aphrodite released a big sigh and let her own emotions show with each and every word. "Honestly I don't really care anymore if they don't worship me, in their own way every time a mortal says, "I love you," and actually means it, it gives me strength. But I refuse to just sit by and watch one of our own brethren destroy something that I believe in and let him destroy something so pure and innocent all because he couldn't get what he wanted like a spoilt child." Her speech left her feeling both empowered and weak and she sagged back against the pillows. She really couldn't care less if Hades approved or not, but she needed him on her side. Whatever Apollo had done she had almost no power and as such had no way to assist Cosmos and Sonia. She looked again at the large god and prayed that he would help.

"I need your help, Hades, I can't do this on my own. Whatever Apollo has planned it will not only affect the mortals in their modern world but our domain as well." Aphrodite let out her worry and concern as well as her hurt. "Hades, what is to stop Apollo doing what he has done to me, to other immortals? He has somehow managed to strip me of my power and in turn this will effect love past, present and future. What if he does this to you or Poseidon or Zeus? That could affect the very makeup of the world."

Hades again resumed his pacing as he mulled over her words, the implications worse than he could have thought.

"If I help you, goddess, I run the risk of pissing off my brother. You have already risked a hell of a lot and I am actually surprised Zeus hasn't already stepped in and stopped all involvement. You know full well how Zeus feels about becoming involved with mortals."

Aphrodite, although weak, fire back. "Well, if he was that concerned why has Apollo been left unchecked? Why should I be penalised for mopping up after that horse's ass?" Aphrodite's shoulders sagged more as her strength started to wane. "So is that a no then? You won't help? I understand but to be honest, Hades, I think it's bullshit."

Hades, as well as her companion, Meton, looked stunned at her use of words and the fact she had directed them at the elder god. Even though she was weak and pale he could see her immortal spark. Only this was more a spark of anger, her use of modern speech showed him how entrenched in the mortal world she had become.

"I beg your pardon?" Hades asked in a quiet, calm voice, still unable to believe she had spoken to him in such a way.

Aphrodite folded her own arms across her chest and lifted her chin.

"I said, oh powerful god of the underworld, bullshit." She let that hang in the air for a few seconds as she watched the god. Meton himself had backed away to a safer distance in preparation for retaliation. "Since when have you been bothered with what Zeus thinks? Neither have you, Zeus or Poseidon seemed bothered about the rules especially when it comes to your own personal lives." Aphrodite knew she was pushing against boundaries but right now she didn't care, there were more important things at stake. "How many demigod children do your brothers have? Yeah, they really abide by the rules."

"DO NOT SPEAK OF WHAT YOU KNOW NOTHING ABOUT, GODDESS!" Hades' voice boomed throughout the chamber. His anger caused his own power to flex and pulse. "We all follow the rules, Aphrodite."

Aphrodite growled and clenched her teeth at the god's condescending tone, she took a page out of Arianna's book and faced down the god.

"Again, bullshit and, yes, I am fully aware I am calling out one of the big bad three. You actually think I don't know Hades, lord of the underworld, protector of lost souls? That I would miss something so obvious?"

Hades looked genuinely confused. Her outburst although expected was now taking a turn and deep down he didn't like the direction.

"I am fucking LOVE incarnate, in the name of the sacred oracle you cannot hide that from me."

Her voice filled the chamber and what little power she had left emanated throughout the room. As daunting as the god was he backed up a step and visibly paled. His voice now quiet and belayed worry.

"You can't know. No one knows. Not even Zeus." He shook his head, this was the only time in the existence of the gods that she had seen him close to being rattled. He was now mumbling to himself as he once again resumed his pacing. "I made sure she couldn't be found; that no deity would be able to sense her."

Aphrodite sighed as her anger vanished. As much as he was a powerful, immortal god he was still just a man, a man who now looked concerned and worried.

"Hades, my lord," she laced her voice with the respect she held for him. "I only know because of who I am, I am Love." She placed her hand on her chest over her own heart. "I am able to see what the heart yearns for the most and yours, my lord, is almost at breaking point."

Hades stopped and looked down again at the goddess as she rested against the pillows on her bed. She had regained some colour but it was still obvious that all was not well. He had been stunned at first that she had openly shouted at him. Then for her to know his deepest secret, well that, in the words of the mortals, knocked the shit out of him. It was as if she had seen straight through him and into the deepest recesses of his heart and soul. It was a feeling he found worrisome and disconcerting. Now it looked like the whole of Olympus would be aware of his single weakness, aware of what he had pined for and what would bring him to his knees and all because he let his heart rule instead of his head.

"So, goddess, what do you plan to do? Tell the whole of Olympus that Hades, ruler of the underworld, is a love struck fool?" His pride would take a huge hit and his brothers would no doubt find it highly entertaining. Them he could and would handle as long as the details of his secret were kept hidden. Aphrodite held up her hand to catch his attention. Her voice clear and with no malice.

"Hades, stop! I will tell no one of this, it is not my secret to tell." She looked around the room and took a few deep breaths before she turned her violet gaze on him. "I need your help, Hades, as I have already said. Help me with this dilemma and in turn I promise, as the goddess of love, to help you." She smiled openly, a smile that showed she meant her word. "I assure you the goddess of love herself is much better than a little love potion."

Hades, not for the first time, was stunned. This goddess was nothing at all like the rest of the immortals. She was willing to put herself at risk for a few mortals and she had given her word to help him and not once had she demanded his help. With an answering smile and a nod Hades conjured a second chair, Meton had slowly ventured back to his perch next to the goddess as soon as he knew any danger had passed. He felt light-hearted even though the task ahead was a difficult one and as he took as seat he spoke.

"Tell me, goddess, did you notice anything strange but familiar about the mortal Cosmos?" Hades again called for his seeing pool and the goddess nodded her approval as she took in the beauty of the basin and stand, its silver craftsmanship shimmered in the light of the room.

"Please, Aphrodite, look and tell me what you now see."

Her eyes widened as she looked into the waters, her eyes flickered from the image shown to the face of Hades and back again — the ramifications were huge.

"Oh, bloody hell!"

Chapter Seventeen

Cosmos woke with a start — his heart rate spiking as his warrior senses went on high alert. His eyes scanned the room and looked for any sign, any sort of danger. As his heart calmed the only sounds that filled the room were that of the clock ticking away and Sonia's soft snores. With a final check of the room Cosmos turned and looked down at the sleeping female, once again he felt that familiar tugging in his chest, his heart changed its rhythm as if it wanted to beat in time with hers. He felt a connection with her that he couldn't deny but it also unnerved him. The memory of his dream flashed through his mind, his mother's words echoed in the dark recesses of his soul. "Love her." Surely she didn't mean Sonia? As beautiful as she was she was a hellcat with a whiplash mouth. She also seemed to harbour an intense dislike for him. Only Zeus himself would know why, he had been nothing but courteous towards her.

The urge to lean over and sweep her fiery red locks away from her face had been a constant ache since the first moment he had seen her and now he finally gave in. His fingers lingered on the skin of her cheek. So soft almost like silk to the touch, the pad of his finger stopped and gently followed the line of a few freckles to her nose. Perfect, that's what she was. A need unlike any he had felt before rose up inside and brought back the vision that they had shared when they had first met and he had grabbed a hold of her. The scene of her naked form undulating under his mouth as he took her pleasure with every breath, forcing the hellcat's compliance with every sweep of his tongue.

His own body reacted in an instant and came alive, his urges became more and more insistent that he wake up his stunning hellcat and show her how that vision would really play out. Cosmos withdrew his hand sharply as if her skin burnt to touch, he stood in one movement and paced over to the window — his fists clenched at his sides, he refused to adjust himself now he was hard as rock. One touch and he knew he wouldn't be able to stop. Her scent, her beauty all of this coupled with his lack of ability in the mosaic had made him aroused beyond reason. Cosmos had some pride left and truthfully he didn't want Sonia to see the animal he would become if he let his darker side take over. She wasn't his, he wasn't sure where that thought had come from and again the whole situation made him uneasy. He took another look at the sleeping redhead before he turned back to the window and moved the blind to look upon this new world. A world where metal beasts ruled the roads, regardless of the hour he watched them speed up and down the street, this world never seemed to stop. The world as he had known it was gone and his heart yearned for the quietness that was his homeland. People milled up and down the street oblivious to the dark shadows that followed them, their steps, more stumbles, made it known that they had partaken in some sort of festivities. A lone shadow pulled Cosmos' gaze — a single figure stood partially hidden by the trunk of a tree, it hovered as if waiting. Cosmos leant forward until his nose nearly touched the glass and his breath fogged the surface. He needed to see better, something about this figure sent his senses into overdrive; they screamed, "Danger! Danger!"

The figure as if pulled by Cosmos' thoughts stepped out from behind the tree's shadows and into the light of the street lamps. Their bright yellow light illuminated a middle aged man with balding hair. He looked ordinary and normal to a passer-by but Cosmos could see the subtle difference that made him stand out, could see what had made the hairs on Cosmos neck stand on end. The male stood and stared straight up at Cosmos, his eyes were a luminescent red and he grinned almost feral like. Cosmos saw straight through the human persona and into its soul. A creature much like the others that he had battled in the park with Arcaeus but this one felt, in Cosmos' gut, even more dangerous. The creature's eyes were filled with malice and hatred and they pinned Cosmos in their snare. This being was the one he had to destroy first and foremost, this one was the one that would be the most danger to Sonia. Cosmos growled in response as the creature backed away and back into the shadows, the challenge had been set.

Cosmos dropped the blind and backed away from the window.

"Zeus's balls!" His voice was harsh in the silence as he turned and looked again down at Sonia. He needed to get Sonia out of this building and into somewhere where he could protect her better. He hated to wake her up as he knew the past few hours had taken their toll as well as the constant pain she must be feeling from the injury in her hand.

Cosmos knelt next to her on the sofa and reached out to cup her cheek, he kept telling himself it was to wake her up alone but he couldn't help but want to touch her.

"Hellcat," he whispered. "Wake up for me." He swept his thumb across her cheek and down to her lips. "Open those beautiful eyes, princess. Come on," he smiled as she started to stir. She stretched a little and unknowingly moved her cheek into his hand, almost seeking his touch. He watched as her eyes fluttered open and revealed her beautiful ocean blue eyes still cloudy with sleep, she looked up at him as his thumb brushed her cheek.

"Hey, hellcat. Wakey, wakey."

She smiled and Cosmos's heart thumped hard in his chest at her smile just before it slowly started to disappear. As the sleep from her eyes vanished it was replaced by confusion. He dropped his hand as she started to sit up, drowsiness was soon replaced by a combination of fear and irritation. In all his years as warrior Cosmos had prided himself on being quick and agile but not today. Faster than a Nemean lion Sonia's fist shot out and connect with his nose.

"Ow!" Cosmos gritted out as he clutched his nose and stood — a steady stream of blood dripped from the appendage and through his fingers as he glared at her. Sonia glared back and slowly moved off the sofa and around the back, eager to move away from the domineering warrior. He now stood to his full height and even though he was in a slight bit of discomfort with his now busted nose he knew he was still a frightening male. His full out glare caused the hairs to rise on her arms and the back of her neck.

Cosmos snorted and then winced as he pushed his nose back into place. Love her? Ha, as if that was going to happen. He watched as she continued to back away from him and opened the distance between them. He growled in response, this Cosmos didn't like, he had been tasked with protecting her and he would do it even if she was going to be a pain in the proverbial ass about it. With another throaty growl he followed until he had backed her into the wall that stood between the kitchen and the hallway. Cosmos wiped his bloodied hand upon his thigh before he moved it upwards to follow his other in caging her in, his hands flexed as they rested next to her head. He fought the pull of her alluring blue eyes but was unable to stop himself from staring at her lips, plump and rosy they begged to be kissed and sucked. Her chest visibly heaved as he bent his head, his nose filled with her perfect scent, vanilla mixed with a hint of lemon, so fresh. His mind became filled with thoughts of possessing her mouth, of making her submit to him. He was a warrior after all. Only an inch separated their mouths, just a little further and he would take what had helped to keep him sane when he had been trapped inside the mosaic. Only an inch left…

Her next words stopped his slow descent and saved his sanity, they reminded him of his mission.

"Get any closer, arsewipe, and I will be replacing your tonsils with your balls."

Cosmos moved his gaze from her lips up to her eyes, anger made the blue pop and sizzle as she glared at him, her cheeks were flushed with irritation but her eyes held just a hint of fear. Did she fear him? Did she think he would hurt her?

With another growl he gritted out, "Pack a bag, hellcat, we are leaving." With a quick glance to her lips once again he pushed off the wall and stalked away from her. His swift strides took him back to the window and without turning he called out, "Now, princess! Unless you want to be here to greet your new guests."

Sonia frowned and attempted without success to get her heart rate under control. Gods, he had been so close to kissing her and she had wanted it. It took everything she had to bark out those bitchy words to make him back up. This male had far too much effect on her. She felt her cheeks flame yet again as she thought of the dream that he had woken her up from. In her dream they had been in the shower together — her body backed into the tiles as he had lifted her up and given her immense pleasure. So close to the edge of the abyss she had awoken to his scent and his hand touching her face. Her body still throbbed, her nipples ached and her panties were soaked. To find him so close and to find it had been only a dream had caused her to react a little harshly. She tried with all of her might to hide her arousal, she didn't need Cosmos to know how close she was to orgasm and she definitely didn't need any of his condescending comments either. The thing is, Sonia acted all bitchy and like she hated his guts but if she was honest with herself only she would admit that this warrior had lit something inside of her. Ever since she had first seen him on that huge piece of stone she had been drawn to him. She had almost given in to her desires when he had caged her against the wall but she knew it was probably all a show to get her to submit to his domineering ways. He didn't like her that was obvious. She had finally been able to take a deep, clear breath when he had stalked away, but now she felt confused at his words as she watched him continuously look through the blinds and out of the window.

"What's the matter?" Sonia asked as she moved towards his position. Emerald green pegged her as she approached. Instead of his growl of annoyance that she was expecting he sighed and wiggled his fingers at her to come closer. As soon as she was within reach he pulled her into his arms and faced her towards the window. His breath whispered across her ear as he lifted up his arm to pull the blind to the side, she shivered but refused to acknowledge her body's reactions, she repeated her question.

"What's wrong?"

Cosmos nodded towards the window where he held the blind slightly to the side. Sonia peered through the gap and out onto the street. Lamps lit the pavement but also illuminated was what the big warrior was concerned about. Sonia was unable to hold in her gasp of shock.

"Oh, god! How did they find us?" She looked again just to confirm what she had seen. The creatures from the park now paced the pavement opposite the building, four of them in total and every now and again they would stop and stare up at window. Sonia stepped back sharply and was stopped by the hard body of Cosmos, she could seem to look away from the creatures as they paced and swayed. She didn't even flinch when Cosmos wrapped his arms around her waist and tugged her away from the window. His voice gentle and quiet he almost carried her back into the centre of the room.

"Come, you must collect your belongings and we must be gone

from here."

Sonia turned and looked up, she knew she looked scared but right now she just didn't care.

"Why are they here, Cosmos?"

Cosmos shook his head and nodded towards her room.

"We will discuss this later." Cosmos turned Sonia and with gentle hands he pushed her towards the door to her room. "Hurry now, hellcat, we haven't much time."

Chapter Eighteen

Devastation watched the coverings on the window twitch as they fell back into place. A grin played at his lips, his master would be pleased. Pleased that they had been able to track the female quickly. Her blood's scent coated his nostrils and the roof of his mouth and left little doubt that he could track her no matter where she may be. Now was the task to lure her away from her warrior protector, lure her away and take her back to the mosaic so his master could complete the ritual, so his brethren could be freed and unleash darkness upon this mortal realm. As a creature born in the deepest darkest recesses of the underworld his nature and urge to maim, kill and torture was dominant. Nothing felt as wonderful to him as the feel of his claws as they sliced through flesh, the way blood would run in rivulets through his hands or the taste of it in his mouth. They were the bringers of death and destruction, demons of the underworld, beings of nightmare. This mortal world would be theirs for the taking. The master had said the female was to be untouched and unharmed — that they would stick to — but he had said nothing about the other mortals that milled about like cattle. With a growl he called to his brethren who paced in front of the stone building that housed the female, he didn't doubt the warrior would move her now that he knew of their presence. In fact he counted on that, he would relish the chase. The creatures gathered around and their grunts and hisses filled the quiet. As if sensing danger, no mortals passed by. They would have their fun and satisfy their needs and then they would hunt. With a final look up at the window he licked his lips.

Devastation they called him in the underworld and soon the mortal world would know the true meaning of the word.

Upon the highest peak of Mount Olympus stood the great temple to the King of gods — Zeus.

The powerful immortal sat not on his dais as would be expected but perched upon the windowsill and looked down over the realm of the immortals. Today he felt old, he felt every one of his long lived years. The cause this time was not the mortals that usually irritated him but his own immortal kind. He could feel the energy that ran through Olympus had changed, its flow and ebb had lost its direction and no longer felt as if it was in control.

A loud sigh filled his chamber; he really didn't need this shit right now. The mortal world had changed dramatically and the gods were no longer the focus of the mortals and as such their powers had become effected. But more than that he needed to find another way for their power to be replenished, if not by worship then by some other means. His fellow gods, whoever it was, needed to cease their meddling before it affected more than just the flow of power. It didn't help they seemed to act like children when they were around each other as well as wanting to get one up on each other. Zeus stood to his full height and stretched, maybe a trip down to the mortal world would be to his advantage, it had certainly been a while since his last visit. At 6ft8 Zeus's form towered above the other gods. Only Hades and Poseidon came even close to his build and size and that was the only thing the mortals' history books had got right. His eyes were a stormy grey that swirled as if a tempest were housed within their depths. His hair so blonde it was almost white and it fell in soft waves to just above his shoulders. Unlike the thousands of depictions the mortals had created, Zeus had no beard. Instead he had a small goatee that went around his lips and chin and showcased a delicious set of lips that were almost feminine in their shape and size yet looked perfect upon him. Zeus's form filled out his toga to perfection, as was expected of any of the gods, especially the great god. Broad shoulders, a wide chest and huge biceps. That along with the obligatory eight-pack and legs that would make any rugby player jealous and woman thinking less than clean thoughts about the power behind them. Zeus was the whole package and he wore it with confidence. It was little wonder women throughout the ages had fallen for his charms.

At this moment Zeus felt anxious and irritable; whatever was messing with the balance of powers had put him in a dark mood. He turned and strolled to his dais. Despite his size he was graceful as he sank into the plush throne.

"Hermes!" Zeus's voice rolled like thunder throughout the temple and lightning filled the skies in answer to the change in mood from the god. As was a habit, Zeus played with a section of hair at the back of his neck. He twirled the lock around his index finger as he became deep in thought. The action was almost mortal in its origins. The flutter of wings filled the chamber and signalled the arrival of Hermes, messenger to the gods. He flew into the room on winged feet, his signatory staff held out in front as he landed just in front of the stairs that led up to the dais. With a long sweep of his hand he bowed so low his head almost touched the floor.

"My lord! You bellowed," his crystal clear voice rang out in the chamber and was laced with a hint of humour. Zeus rolled his eyes, but couldn't stop the small smile that played at his lips.

"Cut it out, Hermes, you know there is no need to do that."

Hermes lifted his head and grinned then stood to his own full height of 6ft5, he pushed his hand through his own golden locks then leant on his staff.

"Ha, I just couldn't resist. The way you were sat there all sullen and broody. It's any wonder the mortals all think you are a moody bastard."

Zeus raised an eyebrow in response. He wasn't that moody was he? He ignored the taunt and simply lifted up his middle finger in response. Hermes barked out a laugh and quickly conjured a chair to recline in.

"Now that, my lord, was not very godlike. So, what can I do you for?" The messenger winked as he leant forward in the chair, his elbows rested on his knees. "Need me to set up that date with Hera yet? You know, considering you two are married." Hermes said this with a smirk as he air-quoted, 'uarried'. "You two really need to, you know, talk or maybe be in the same room."

Zeus liked Hermes and felt he could be himself around the god, plus they had both spent a lot of time around mortals in the past so they were the least formal out of all of the gods. Well, to each other that was. He would probably get reprimanded by some of the more traditional immortals if they ever caught him. Especially goddesses like Demeter.

"Seriously, Hermes, is that all you got? You've been using that line for years. I can't help it if she hates me and I'm fucked if I know what I did to warrant that hate. I've always been nice to her." He placed his own hands on his knees and copied Hermes' pose. "Anyway, that isn't why I called you."

The messenger sat back and smiled, his straight white teeth almost matched the marble work, his eyes a bright emerald tinged with silver sparkled with intelligence and cunningness.

"Zeus, come on, she caught you with a nymph so you need to put up and apologise or else you are so not getting any…ever…again." He grinned some more and continued, "So, what do you need?"

Zeus sat back in his dais and rested his beefy arms on the sides, his face turned serious.

"Can you tell me where my brothers are right now at this moment?" He didn't tell Hermes why he needed to know, he would keep that to himself for now. For starters he wanted to make sure the issues that were happening weren't due to his brothers thinking they want the throne again. So he wanted to cross them off his list.

Zeus watched as Hermes closed his eyes and held out his right hand. One of his gifts was being able to locate any of the gods at any given time. Over his hand sand poured out onto an invisible flat surface, the sand spread out and moved almost as if it was floating in water until peaks and troughs formed. Soon the image took on the shapes of temples until even trees and bushes could be seen. A complete detailed map of Mount Olympus now hovered above the hand of Hermes. Dotted across the surface were bright coloured lights, he opened his eyes and they glowed from the use of his power.

"Ok, so Poseidon is currently in his playhouse in Atlantium; I think I heard he had a demigod issue to deal with. One of his sons went a tad AWOL and created a tsunami," Hermes rolled his eyes and shrugged. He eyed the coloured lights quickly identifying who was who.

Both gods bent their heads to study the map and Zeus pointed towards an indigo coloured light.

"Is that Hades?" Hermes smacked the back of Zeus' hand with his left.

"Don't bloody touch it and yes it is, from the looks of things he is in the temple of love with Aphrodite and her companion, Meton," Hermes pointed out the pink and pale green lights. "But this doesn't seem right."

Zeus watched as Hermes leant in closer and frowned. "What's wrong, Hermes?"

Hermes pointed again at the pink light that signalled Aphrodite. "This here usually is bright pink and now it's pale and almost diminished."

Zeus straightened as he turned and walked back towards the window to look out over his domain. He placed his hands upon the windowsill and sighed hard, his head bowed. This just proved what his gut feeling was telling him. Something was wrong, something was effecting the energies. Without turning he called out, his voice tired.

"Tell me, my friend, do any of the other lights appear the same as Aphrodite's?"

Zeus could hear the other god stand and pace closer as he looked the map in his hand. His answer was quick.

"No, none of the others show the same level as energy as her, it's as if she has been drained."

Zeus nodded and then turned, he folded his arms across his chest, "That will be all for now, Hermes, please keep me posted on the others and if you notice the same thing let me know."

Hermes nodded and went to turn.

"Hermes! Don't tell any of the others either, let's keep this between us."

The messenger nodded again.

"Yes, Zeus," he said then took a breath and blew across his palm, like sand on a beach the map vanished into the air. "I will be awaiting your summons, my lord." With a smile Hermes lifted into the air, again the sound of wings filled the chamber as he left Zeus to his own thoughts. Zeus looked again at the realm of Olympus, his gaze quickly found the temple of Love. Zeus hated this situation and felt like things were speeding out of his control, he would delay his trip into the mortal world and would first go and see what had called Hades' attention in the temple of Aphrodite. Maybe, just maybe, he would get some answers.

Chapter Nineteen

Cosmos gripped his seat like a vice and clenched his teeth — this was not how he wanted to travel to get away from those creatures. He would have rather battled with them then ride in this contraption. He looked over at Sonia and watched as she gripped the wheel in front of her, steering the 'car' as she called it. Car sounds better than, 'my little pocket rocket,' whatever that meant. What the hell ever happened to horses? At least he was always in control when he rode them, every time he turned to watch the world pass by in the car he was overcome with nausea. So instead he watched Sonia, he watched the way she kept her eyes glued to the road in front and the fact she wore a constant frown as if she was deep in thought.

It had only been a day since he had been freed and had met the red haired beauty but it had felt like so much longer. The more time he spent with her the more he felt as if destiny or fate had pushed it to be. He no longer saw her as an issue that needed sorting. She was just as innocent in this as the other mortals that would become caught up in the gods' meddling. He sounded like a lovesick fool when he thought of all the many things he was coming to enjoy about Sonia. The way her name rolled off his tongue, her quick wit and hellfire tongue, as well as the fact she took no shit from anyone, even him.

What impressed him the most was her ability to deal with the current situation. She had taken it all in her stride and just rolled with it even though she had no idea what to make of him or the creatures and had no idea that the gods and the magic were in fact real. Her voice pulled Cosmos from his thoughts.

"Stop staring at me." Her eyes stayed glued to the road before her. Cosmos grinned and turned only slightly in his seat to face her, his thigh brushed against her own and he didn't miss the catch in her breath as it did.

"I like staring at you, Sonia, it's much more pleasant than watching the scenery fly by." He would not reveal that as he looked at her the urge to empty his stomach had vanished. She already had a low regard for him and he refused to let it get any lower. He couldn't help but want to rile her up a bit, she was even more beautiful when she looked flushed with anger.

"Why do you frown so much Hellcat?" He tilted his head as he said this. He then watched as she flicked her gaze towards him and frowned harder.

"Stop it, it's annoying." She didn't answer his question but he knew she was losing her patience with him so he pushed.

"That frown does not become you, hellcat. You going to tell me what ails you?" Cosmos rested his arm across the back of her driving seat, he felt confined in this damned machine, his knees were nearly at his chest as he was squished into the seat.

She flicked her gaze again at him but this time it lingered a little longer, he had noticed that she would sneak glances at his form whenever she thought he wouldn't notice. But he did, mainly because he watched her just as much. Cosmos had always prided himself on being straight to the point and so he would be. He wanted to know how she felt, especially about him.

"You like what you see? Mayhap later on I could show you more. I will admit it's been a while for me with being trapped but I do believe all the important equipment still works. Although, at times, a certain area still feels as if it is as hard as stone." He grinned more and watched for her reaction.

Sonia spluttered and steered the car sharply, the wheels nearly hitting the curb.

"What?" Her gazed flew from him and back to the road continuously.

Cosmos continued, "I said do you like what you see? If so, hellcat, we can arrange some time later on where you can look your fill and mayhap even touch if that is what you wish."

"No, I do not wish it and I won't be looking either. Dammit, what is wrong with you?" Sonia slammed her hands into the steering wheel and kept her eyes straight in front. Cosmos this time frowned and watched the change of emotions cover her face. Was he wrong? Did she not like his body, did she really hate him? He turned back again in his chair and faced forward, he never usually had any issues with women, yet this one really did seem to hate him. He openly looked again across to see her flick her gaze back to the road, once they had stopped the machine he would find out. She couldn't keep her eyes off him, so why did she deny herself? Her body would tell him the truth and, oh, how he planned to take his time in getting that question answered.

Cosmos searched deep down inside where his gut instinct resided, down in that place where he felt his magic rested. He reached and took a hold then freed it, it had been many a year since he had let his gift free but now it told him what he needed to know. Sonia was his, the gods had seen fit to tie their fates. Their auras pulled at each other in a bid to merge, to mate. His soul had known the answer as soon as he had touched her and it was the reason his heart already beat in time with her own. Too fast some might say, but fate worked in its own way and would not be denied. Cosmos closed his eyes and gave a silent thanks to the gods. He would protect Sonia — that had always been the plan — but now he had a greater purpose, by fate she was his and Cosmos would do all he could to make her see that.

His hellcat.

His soulmate.

Sonia was confused, confused as hell at the male sat next to her. She gripped the steering wheel of her Mini harder and attempted to not sneak peeks at him every other second. What in god's name was wrong with him? He had basically just offered himself to her, that's if she understood his innuendo correctly. The minute he had repeated the offer her mind had taken a hold and gone into overdrive with thoughts and mental images that all focused on his smooth, tanned extremely muscly skin. Sonia licked her lips. All that just for her, damn.

To make matters worse when he had described that certain area to being 'like stone' it had hit her right in the lady garden and caused an answering clench and throb. Sonia focused her thoughts back on the road and tried her hardest to keep herself from mounting the curb — she smirked to herself. That would be the only mounting she would be doing for the next few hours. She shook her head; she really didn't understand Cosmos at all. Talk about mixed messages, she was starting to get whiplash from the to-ing and fro-ing. He had been quite hostile towards her when they had first met and now all of a sudden he had changed. Since they had left the apartment he had been constantly throwing glances her way. Like now she could feel his eyes on her. She had told a blatant lie when she had told him it was annoying, in fact it felt the complete opposite. Every time he turned those green orbs on her, her body reacted; she felt a blush creep over her skin and her heart rate would pick up ever so slightly. The problem she was having was that every time he did her mind would think it was ok to visit those dreams and visions that she had had of them together. Driving her car was now becoming more and more difficult. She was actually afraid to pull over as she was convinced her body would take over and be across the gear stick and into his lap in a heartbeat.

"Sonnie, you really need to get a bloody grip," she mumbled and shook her head a little. As soon as the sounds had left her mouth she felt that familiar gaze return, his warm honey laced words filled the car.

"Hellcat, what's wrong?"

"Nothing, Cosmos, I'm fine," she lied again. "Why do you call me that?" Sonia blurted out before her brain could engage. She peeked at him again from the corner of her eyes. Did she really want to know the answer? He probably thought she was something from hell with the way she had spoken to him. She waited with her breath held for him to answer, her shoulders steeled ready.

"Because you are fiery, Sonia, it's in your nature. Fire is passion." When he said her name with his slight accent her heart reacted and her body tingled as goosebumps erupted across her skin.

"What!? I'm not fiery, I'm just opinionated," Sonia was unable to hold back her retort. Cosmos laughed, his voice smooth as it filled the car. Sonia could do little but shoot glares in his direction every now and again.

"Oh, Sonia, a hellcat indeed. Put your claws away for now, I meant no disrespect."

Sonia heard the creak of the leather in his seat as he moved. His size easily filled out his side of the car but he was still able to manoeuvre himself and close the distance even more without obstructing her driving. She felt his breath next to her ear and then the light touch of his fingers as he moved a lock of hair away from her face.

"Oh, hellcat, I can't tell you how much your flushed skin affects me so," his breath was warm and his scent, all woodsy and male, filtered into her senses. "Like stone, remember?" He chucked quietly, "I do wonder whether you can go from hellcat to hummingbird with the right persuasion."

Sonia found it continuously difficult to focus on the road, she tried her best to concentrate on the car in front and on keeping on her side of the road. Her knuckles had turned white as she gripped the steering wheel. The force caused pain to shoot from her palm. Sonia's voice was just a whisper.

"Cosmos, please stop."

She felt his breath leave her cheek and heard the squeak of leather as he returned to his previous position. Arm raised holding onto the strap above the door and eyes focused out of the window.

"For now, Sonia. For now," his voice was just as quiet as her own but the words were more powerful then she expected.

Another peak out of the corner of her eye, she watched Cosmos reached just under his leather kilt and she felt her eyes widen. Her eyes continued to flick back from the road to him. The kilt lifted and revealed a thigh that bulged with muscle. Sonia's mouth went dry and her eyes moved up the thigh to where his hand had vanished and adjusted a very obvious huge erection.

"Oh, good lord," she whispered under her breath and forced her eyes to stay in front whilst her body pulsed with need and her heart sounded loud in her ears. They had another hour to go before they would arrive at her grandmother's cottage. In that time she was positive that she would spontaneously combust. A few deep breaths in and out and she attempted to speak again.

"We need to make a stop on the way. We will need some food and…" She paused and looked over at him and met his gaze. "We need to get you some different clothes, you kinda stick out a bit"

His own gaze was soft and he nodded and smiled a little.

"As you wish, hellcat. As you wish."

Sonia nodded back. She had expected a fight so she was pleasantly surprised he had just agreed.

"Sonia?" She looked again as he called her name quietly.

"Yes, Cosmos."

"You may clothe me but I would rather Hades himself drag my soul back to the underworld than be subjected to wearing those garments Arcaeus told me were called underwear, so please do not bother."

He nodded again and then turned to look out of the passenger window, Sonia had almost relaxed until she heard his next words and nearly choked on fresh air.

"I swear to Zeus himself I will not let my love plums be strangled."

Sonia coughed and he smiled at her as he realised he had been heard.

"Love plums? Who the hell did you get that from?"

Cosmos shrugged, "Arcaeus. He said that it was the right thing to say when talking of one's balls." He shrugged again and didn't say any more.

Sonia looked forward and blinked, he words more automatic as her mind just gave up, "Oh, ok then."

Chapter Twenty

"Arcaeus, honey?" Arianna yawned and called out. She was still tucked tightly under the quilt in her bed. The only thing missing was her man. It felt strange for him not to be by her side. Even though they had only been together a short while in this time, their souls had always been together. The minute they separated her heart missed him and yearned for his return. Most people, especially in the modern world, would snort and tell her she was being stupid and talking shit but Arianna knew what she felt deep inside.

"Arcaeus!" Arianna called out again and threw back the covers. She shivered as she placed her feet into her slip-ons and climbed off the bed, she yawned again as she reached the bedroom door and gently opened it to peek into the hallway. A look towards the lounge told her he wasn't there or even in the kitchen as the apartment was too quiet. A small snore caught her attention and brought her gaze towards the hallway near the front door. She covered her mouth to yawn again as she looked down upon the man of her dreams, literally. She had been so exhausted when they had arrived home in the early hours that once she had gotten into bed she had passed out without realising Arcaeus hadn't gotten into bed with her. Her male had spent most of the night barricading the front door and had promptly fallen asleep propped up in front of it. His sword rested across his lap, his right hand still gripped the hilt. Behind her warrior and against the front door he had placed her spare set of drawers from the spare room as well as other heavy items he had placed on the top.

Arianna smiled and padded quietly towards him — her warrior, always the protector, had taken it upon himself to make sure she was protected. She honestly didn't think she could love him any more than she did right now. Her heart felt full to brimming with love. One of those stupid sayings kept repeating in her head, going round and round, 'You can take the man out of the battle, but you can't take the battle out of the man." She knelt next to him and with gentle fingers she stroked down his cheek and across his lips, her face so close she could smell his breath that was laced with coffee he had obviously been drinking whilst he had been on guard.

"Arcaeus, my love." Her whispered words were cut off as a hand clamped onto her throat and she was thrown onto her back. She gasped and grabbed at the hand as she tried to call out. Her heart thundered against her chest as she looked up into Arcaeus' eyes. They were clouded with sleep but the ferocity in them scared her. As she clutched at the hand clamped around her throat she croaked out his name in an attempt to get through to him.

"Arcaeus… Please… It's me… Anya."

"Oh fuck! Arianna!"His eyes changed the instant he recognized his mistake his hand immediately lifted from her throat and to her face, remorse so deep was etched across his face as he leant closer to her. "Oh god, baby. I'm so sorry, did I hurt you? Anya, talk to me." The desperation laced in Arcaeus' voice pulled Arianna from her shocked daze. She knew he had never meant to hurt her and he had just been reacting to the moment. It was her own fault for disturbing him whilst he was on guard. Arianna lifted her hands and placed them over his, her fingers stroked the skin on the back of his hand.

"Arcaeus, I'm fine." She looked up into his eyes and smiled, "Honest, I'm ok." She squeezed his hands reassuringly. He didn't answer but ran his eyes all over her face, they brimmed with mortification with what he had done. In frantic movements he cupped her face with both hands and tipped it from side to side, his brown eyes searched for any sign of his rough handling.

"Arcaeus, stop it. I'm ok. Please." Her stern voice echoed loudly within the hall as Arcaeus removed his hands from Arianna's face and sat back; a deep frown marred his forehead as he bent it as if ashamed to look her into her eyes.

"I'm fine, baby, honest. No harm done, ok?" Arianna leant up on her elbows and continued on. "You didn't hurt me okay, Maybe shocked the shit out of me," she smiled as he raised his eyes to look at her. "I shouldn't have touched you when you were on guard and asleep." Arianna reached out a hand to him. "Old habits die hard, hey, my warrior?"

Arcaeus took her hand and followed when she tugged him back towards her, she lay back down as Arcaeus caged her head between his arms. His face so close she could still see the worry etched in his eyes.

"Shit, Anya, I can't apologise enough." He leant down and kissed her forehead before he rested his cheek against her own, his hands finding hers and bringing them up above her head, fingers entwined.

"I was dreaming," he continued, his voice a whisper. "I was back in the underworld and on the fields of punishment. I was battling to get back to you but every time I beat one of those creatures you seemed further away." Arcaeus shook his head and kissed her cheek again, his fingers caressed the skin of her hands. "When you touched me I just reacted thinking you were one of them."

Arianna listened to every word and felt his pain as if it were her own but she kept quiet and let him release his worry and concerns.

"Those creatures, baby… When I told you to leave in the park and I faced off with them it was like I was back there. Shit!" He squeezed his eyes shut and brought his head back and as he looked down he opened his eyes again, they shined with unshed tears. "Please forgive me," his voice cracked as he released her hands to cup Anya's cheeks again. "Forgive me, baby, please. You know that there isn't a force on this earth or Olympus itself that would be able to keep me from reaching you." Arcaeus then bent his head until their lips were separated by a breath. "I would battle those things a hundred times over and defeat the fucking lot if I knew you would be there waiting for me at the end."

Arianna's heart beat like the clappers as she smiled up at Arcaeus, she lifted her arms from behind her and wrapped them around his neck.

"Arcaeus, there is nothing to forgive"

His answering smile stunned Arianna. "Our souls were destined, fated to be together. No mortal or gods would deny that, my Anya."

Arcaeus bent and pressed his lips gently to Arianna's and swept his tongue across her plump lower one, she tightened her hold around his neck and tugged. This action pulled him into the cradle of her body, her legs immediately wrapped around his waist. Her voice whispered again.

"I forgive you, Arcaeus, my love, my heart." She sucked his lower lip and tugged then smiled as she released it with a pop. "It would take more than the gods to keep us apart… I love you."

No further words were needed as their lips met again, this time the passion they held for one another freed. Safe and sound behind Arcaeus' barricade and so entranced in each other that neither one heard the muffled message tones of their mobile phones.

Chapter Twenty-One

"My lady, do you require another drink?" Meton's concerned voice once again filled the chamber, but right now his voice and that of Hades' irritated the hell out of her. Aphrodite brought her fingertips to her head and started to massage her temples gently with small circles of her fingertips. Yes, she still felt like death and she was positive she looked like Cerberus had used her as a chew toy. Well, not as bad as that, she was love after all and that being said she would always look half decent. She was still reclined on her bed in her chambers as ordered by her companion and to her surprise Hades. He had taken all the information on board and was now running the show. Now she had to deal with either him or Meton coming in every ten minutes to check on her. Aphrodite kept her voice as neutral as possible as she answered

"No, Meton. Thank you but I am fine."

A flutter of wings signalled Meton's departure from the chamber. As he returned to his spot next to Hades in the antechamber they continued their discussion on ways to halt the drain on her power and to find out how Apollo had done it. She was surprised with how involved and intense Hades had become in helping her, but then again she had promised to help Hades end his millennia of loneliness.

Maybe, just maybe, that was incentive enough. She herself had continuously gone over and over the events that had happened and tried to figure out how he had done it. But so far all they knew was that Apollo had managed to tap into Aphrodite's energies and was now slowly syphoning them. It was worrying indeed when she was replenished with love, so she now felt like a live battery for her arsehole brother's needs.

She could feel the pull as whatever was draining her took more. Every time she felt weaker than before no matter how much love itself eased into her. Each time a true soulmate was found or true love was admitted a small flow of energy filtered back into her. But it wasn't enough. Other worries had also started to surface like her protection charms, especially the one she had placed over Arianna and Arcaeus. She hoped deep down that her powers in that respect had not been affected and she prayed that they were still invisible to Apollo.

Loud voices pulled the goddess from her thoughts; they were muffled but loud enough for her to wince. It was easy to recognise the calming voice of her companion and the deep husky growl of Hades, but the new third voice she just couldn't pinpoint. The voices became louder and clearer as they made their way into the chamber. Aphrodite sat up in her bed and smoothed down her chiton before she faced the newcomer. She should have been surprised but she was actually glad at the male that stood before her.

"Zeus! My lord, you honour me with your presence," Aphrodite bowed her head in respect to the king of the gods.

"No need for the pomp and circumstance, goddess. I'm in no mood to be formal."

As the goddess raised her eyes she was shocked to find Zeus dressed not in his white godly wrappings but as a mortal. She would have had to have been blind not to appreciate how sinfully sexy he currently looked. Dressed in faded blue jeans and a plain white t-shirt he literally radiated power and masculinity. Aphrodite felt a twang of pity for any mortal female that crossed this god's path.

"Zeus, again welcome. I apologise, I am unprepared for your visit." Aphrodite made an effort to move from her reclined position.

"Goddess, stop. Stay where you are and rest," Hades' gentle voice halted her as he walked towards her bed and nodded towards Zeus. "I have already notified Zeus on what has transpired."

At this the goddess winced slightly, her interfering with mortals was a huge no, no. It was one of the main rules of Olympus but they all did it in some way or another. You just didn't throw it in Zeus' face and expect him to like it.

"Relax, goddess, I am not here to reprimand you. I have a small understanding of the details, I think the most important matter is the why and especially how to stop your current ailment from getting any worse." And with that Zeus started to pace, his strides and demeanour almost identical to his brother's. His voiced filled the room. "Are you both definitely sure Apollo is at the heart of this matter?" Zeus shook his head. "What the hell is going through that idiot's mind?"

Both Hades and Aphrodite nodded, the god of the underworld was the first to answer.

"Yes, brother. From what I could see the energy drain is coming directly from one of his enchantments. What confuses me is why he hasn't tried harder to cover his tracks as it were."

This time Aphrodite watched as both elder gods paced, their foreheads creased in matching frowns as they both sunk deep in thought. They were a contrast: one light, one dark, but both devastatingly handsome. This time Aphrodite found her voice and used it to grab their attention.

"He is either being an arrogant ass or he is unaware that it has happened. I think it has been a long time since you have dealt with him and you have forgotten what he is like."

Both males stopped and faced her, their frowns deepened.

"How can he not know? He is a god and he should be aware of his magics, be them small or large." Zeus' naïaa question made Aphrodite blurt out.

"Bullshit! He knows only what interests him or benefits him. He is THAT self-obsessed that he can't see past his own ego." Aphrodite sat up in bed and folded her arms across her ample chest. "But if he finds out that he is capable of draining any one of us, what's to stop him from trying it on you elder gods?" The goddess sagged back into the cushions and sighed, she reached up to rub her temples and garnered worried looks from the brothers.

"Goddess, how are you able to concentrate when you are obviously very weak?" Hades moved back to her bedside and perched on the edge of the large bed and took her small cold hands in his own.

Aphrodite answered, her voice was quiet yet still held an edge of power to it.

"Love, my dear Hades," she smiles weakly. "We may not be worshipped like we used to but love, especially true love, a kind that is found between soulmates. That is what is keeping me alive. As dark and dreary as the world can be there will always be love."

The rustle of feathers drew Aphrodite's attention to her companion as he glided back into the chamber. His golden eyes met her own as he landed near to her bedside.

"My lady, you are well?"

She smiled again and she pulled her hands from Hades' gentle grasp and stroked his feathered head.

"I am fine, Meton, worry not. Please, I ask that you assist both Zeus and Hades, my friend. Sonia and Cosmos will need our help more than ever."

Meton nodded then answered, his calming voice and instant balm to Aphrodite's permanent headache, "Yes, of course, my lady."

"Thank you, Meton. I will close my eyes now, make sure they have all they need." Aphrodite turned her head into the cushions and sighed, sleep pulled and tugged. Oblivion a breath away, Aphrodite fought it as she felt the tug on her energy, but this time it was accompanied by screams, blood curdling screams of the mortals now filled her pain laced mind. Before she succumbed to the blessed darkness she whispered, "He attacks again, no mortal will be safe… Devastation has been unleashed."

Hades' eyes widened as he looked from the unconscious form of Aphrodite to the equally shocked Zeus.

"Zeus, this isn't good. You remember who Devastation is don't you?"

Zeus moved closer to the bed and Aphrodite, he looked upon her form almost seeing through her and beyond as his thoughts raced. He noticed how pale the goddess had become, the pallor of her skin slightly blue and a slight sheen coated the surface.

"Yes, I remember. You have kept that creature trapped within the bowels of Tartarus for over a millennia. How is it Apollo has managed to free him?"

Hades shook his head as he bent and took hold of Aphrodite's hand; in a move too gentle for the lord of the underworld he placed it underneath the covers and tucked her in. Her breathing was slow and deep but her eyelids twitched furiously as her dreams took hold.

"Apollo must have found a way to access the souls of the

underworld, more specifically the fields of punishment and the pits of Tartarus. But it takes more than a simple letting of blood to free a being like Devastation. It takes a full sacrifice."

Hades stood and faced his brother, his own face hidden a little. His eyes brimmed with anger. "Apollo has crossed that line and killed for the sake of his own gain."

Both gods casted a final look at the goddess that had been caught up in a race for her life before they both strode from the room. Happy that her companion, Meton, had remained at her bedside and would call for them if her condition changed and worsened.

"But if he has managed to free that one creature how is it he has not freed the rest of the higher creatures?"

They stepped onto the balcony that overlooked the temple gardens, the occupants that included nymphs and satyrs relaxed and enjoyed the day, unaware of the drama that took place. Hades sighed and leant his muscled arms upon the balcony.

"Only the blood of the Oracle of Delphi has that ability."

Zeus' eyes widened again as he pieced everything together.

"Ahh, shit!" Zeus scribed his hands down his face. "So if he gets his hands on the Oracle and does the unthinkable, he will unleash the fields of punishment and Tartarus upon the mortal world?"

Hades didn't answer verbally — only a nod confirmed Zeus' guess. He clenched his hands around the railings of the balcony. "You mentioned the Oracle is currently being protected… by who?"

Hades continued to look out over the gardens, his thoughts rampant in his head, his words quiet. "Cosmos, the warrior Cosmos is currently at her side. But it is no longer that simple, there is something else you should know and I don't even think Apollo is aware of this." The brothers both turned and faced each other; swirling grey met with royal blue.

"What is it, Hades?"

Hades' voice was clear but again almost too quiet for Zeus to hear, "Cosmos isn't completely mortal."

"What do you mean he isn't mortal?" Zeus frowned and crossed his arms over his chest. "Spit it out already, Hades."

"Cosmos is demigod, Zeus," Hades rushed out.

"So?" Zeus shrugged. "There are plenty of those hanging about." Zeus eyed Hades before blurting out, "He isn't one of mine is he?"

Considering the dire situation Hades couldn't hold back the snort of laughter at the almost panicked look in Zeus's eyes.

"No, brother, as much of a man whore that you are, this one definitely isn't one of yours."

Zeus sagged with relief. "Then who? Bloody hell, Hades, come on."

Hades faced his brother and calmly stated, "It's Apollo." Hades waited for the penny to drop before he continued. "Cosmos is the son of Apollo."

His proclamation was met with stunned silence and he watched as Zeus's mouth opened and closed like that of a koi carp before he turned and again leant on the railing.

"Fuck me that complicates shit."

Hades laughed again but this time it was laced with concern.

"Oh yes, great king of the gods, it does indeed."

Chapter Twenty-Two

Sonia dumped the shopping bags into the boot of the car and leant forward and blew out a breath.

"Come on, girl, that wasn't so bad was it?"

No, it hadn't been bad at all except for the swarms of women that had followed them around the supermarket thinking they had found a star from a movie. Sonia couldn't blame them at all, Cosmos' entire look screamed *300* only without that huge sweeping red cape. It had gotten old real fast and even getting Cosmos changed into modern clothing hadn't changed the reaction of the women. His now modern look didn't take anything away from his masculinity — it actually added to it and then times it by ten. Now dressed in a dark blue jeans and a plain royal blue sweater she found it increasingly hard to focus; that and the fact she knew full well that he wore no underwear under those jeans meant her imagination was running wild. With a final knock of her head Sonia pulled back and slammed the lid closed on the boot and headed around to the driver's side of the car. She had to pull herself together but there was something about the warrior that called out to her. Sonia slid into the driver's seat, avoided a glance in his direction and instead focused on starting the car.

"Sonia? Tell me, how can this material be so soft?"

Sonia left the car to idle and turned in her seat to face the warrior who sat caressing his sweater like he had found the finest fur on earth. His face was a picture of fascination and awe and Sonia had to fight the urge to giggle, instead an unladylike snort escaped and as such pulled Cosmos' attention to her. His look pulled at Sonia's heart strings but her amusement was quick to disappear as she remembered how much she took for granted in this world. He was so new to everything and would find the simplest thing amazing. Sonia smiled and shocked herself by reaching over to grab his large hand, she squeezed it a little and smiled.

"I'm sorry, Cosmos, I forgot you have never seen things like this before. But I assure you it is made the same way as your other clothing, just the material is different."

His lips tilted into a small smile that was heart stopping and caused an answering flutter in Sonia's stomach. Men that were made as gorgeous as him surely should be illegal, any woman with a pulse would find him irresistible. With that in mind Sonia frowned as a small thread of jealousy hit.

"Thank you, Sonia, for understanding. Your world is so new and unusual to me, it is all so fascinating." He grinned as he smoothed the material of his sweater again down the length of his torso, each muscle of his chest and abs still defined. "Now, when will you let me steer this metal beast?"

Sonia coughed and her breath caught in the back of her throat, "Metal beast?" He just grinned again and nodded. "Oh, you mean the car?" He answered again with a nod but this time he brimmed with concealed excitement.

"Yes, I am no longer worried it will harm me and I find the prospect of high speed as Arcaeus explained to me to be eating at my curiosity."

Sonia's hand was now clutched within Cosmos' own callused palm. Its size totally engulfed her own and his thumb had started to rub across her knuckles in a way that distracted her and made her aware of how close they were in the confined space.

"Will you teach me, Sonia?" His voice had dropped lower in tone and Sonia had to fight against the overwhelming need to move closer. With a will she had dredged up from deep inside, she pulled her hand away and placed it onto the steering wheel, her fingers flexed to try and rid herself of his touch that seemed to linger. Her eyes moved away and she faced the view up front, they still had a small way to travel until they reached her grandma's cottage.

"Hellcat?" his voice asked questioningly. She had forgotten she never answered his plea for her to teach him how to drive.

"Yes, Cosmos, I will teach you if that's what it is you want"

His whoop of delight broke the tension that had filled the car and Sonia was finally able to draw a deep breath. If that was how he got his way Sonia would be in trouble if he started to use his charms for other things. There hadn't been many men in her life that could make her feel like she had lost all control and Cosmos was ranking high up as the best. It took Sonia a moment to realise he had continued to talk, going on and on about being able to outdo Arcaeus. His voice with that sexy accent caused shivers to race down her spine. Men! Sonia grinned and thought to herself that no matter the era in time they never changed, they always wanted a pissing contest. Sonia put the Mini into gear and slowly pulled out of the parking space. Luckily the car park and traffic was light so she made it onto the main road quickly to continue their journey.

The silence that filled the car felt surprisingly easy and Sonia found she only noticed the tension was when Cosmos focused his entire being on her. Her eyes, all of their own accordance, fired small glances in his direction. Her whole body tuned to him. A part of her wanted to stop fighting the obvious attraction she had for this larger than life warrior but her fears of rejection held her back and the fact her feelings were happening with a speed she wasn't comfortable with. She wanted to stop overthinking things and go with the flow just like she had done when she had met with other men — just enjoy the moment. But Sonia had a distinct gut feeling that if she let her barriers down and let the warrior in, even a fraction, her heart would never recover the backlash.

Cosmos was on edge, he had been on edge ever since he had been left alone with his hellcat. If it wasn't for his training as a warrior he wouldn't have been able to stop himself from taking her in his arms as soon as he had seen her eyes blaze with obvious jealously in the supermarket when the other women had looked at him with open lust in their eyes. Her reaction showed him that she wasn't as unaffected by him as she had acted and it gave him hope that she was fighting her attraction to him. That he could battle. He would wear down her defences just like he did an enemy in battle. He wanted nothing more than to take her in his arms and make her admit that she wanted him just as much as he had started to want her. His idea to ask for lessons in driving this beast they travelled in had worked in the sense that it had eased the growing tension a little, but he would be glad when they stopped and he was able to get out of the tight confines.

Cosmos leant his head back against the seat and thought back to the fight with the creatures. It was either that or focus on how Sonia's creamy skin called out for his touch. He had found it strange how the creatures hadn't attacked on mass, instead separating off. From his time in the mosaic he had found they were highly aggressive and would attack with little or no provocation, almost mindless and quick to dispatch, if you had the skill. What pulled his concern the most was the creature that had been housed within the body of the mortal. That was not one of the mindless creatures, this one was intelligent and held a malice in its eyes that had promised pain. A muscle in Cosmos' jaw ticked. The creatures weren't after him, they hunted Sonia. He knew the cut on her hand had freed them but he didn't know why they still wanted her. That was something he would have to find out and do his utmost to stop them for their goal.

As a child Cosmos had been taught honour, courage as well as the need to protect those that were weaker. His mother had told stories of how he had been born to protect the innocent and to fight monsters. He had spent a long time thinking his mother had told those stories to give him confidence but now, especially after his time in the underworld and in the mosaic, he had started to believe her. He felt it deep down that he was a protector, his instincts doubled in intensity whenever he thought of Sonia and he would swear to Zeus himself that he would keep her safe, even at the cost of his own life. Cosmos smiled. His mother had always said he was proud and strong like his father; he had no memory of that man but he had always dreamt she was right. His only father figure had been Arcaeus' father who had instilled a sense of integrity into him.

He closed his eyes as Sonia started to sing along to the device she called a radio. It filtered a strange type of music into the cabin and her voice matched along with it, the soothing tones helped calm his heartbeat and easily sent him into a relaxed state. It didn't surprise him the effect she had on him — not only a witch of some sort but it looked like she was a siren as well, one that called out to him on every level. He let her voice float across his nerves and didn't fight the pull to slumber.

Chapter Twenty-Three

Apollo paced the small stage that sat in front of the screen in the small intimate cinema. Only a few patrons had been present when the freed creatures led by the demon, Devastation, had crawled inside and started their own small party. Hades would be on the receiving end of a few new souls tonight. Not that Apollo cared, he didn't even care that the creatures had and would continue to create chaos in this pathetic mortal world. But what had him pacing was the fact that after his direct order they had managed to let that female escape and leave the warrior alive. Now he would have to use more of his power to find out where she was and that would take even more time, time he didn't have. Time was running out and he needed that female back to the mosaic before the portal he had created closed completely. It was either get her back and spill every last drop of her Oracle blood or wait and start again on the next full moon. Apollo stopped his pacing and glared down at the creatures. Waiting wasn't an option, he wasn't known as a patient god and he could feel his nerves start to fray. Apollo bent his head first to the right and then the left hearing a satisfying crack as the bones crunched against each other. The creatures looked up at him, those that watched him back swayed to and fro whilst the others finished gorging themselves on the fallen mortals. Sounds of ripping flesh accompanied that of growling. They had been birthed in the dark recesses of the underworld, deep in the depths of Tartarus.

If Apollo had any light feelings left he would have regretted his actions to bring these beasts forward and release them upon the mortal world. He could still recall the damage they had done that last time they had been allowed free reign and it had taken the powers of all three of the elder gods to seal them away in their prison. That had been over a few millennia ago and it actually made Apollo smile that he might actually cause some chaos to the prim and proper gods. That small part that should regret his past and present decisions was buried deep inside and there would be little chance it could recover. The damage to him was too great to go back to the way things had been. He no longer cared about how the others dealt with the aftermath of this little excursion, all he wanted was his revenge to those that had wronged him. So if the mortals got in his way so be it; they were after all dispensable. It was nothing more than a means to an end.

His golden eyes swept again over the hunched forms of the creatures before connecting with the unflinching gaze of Devastation. A true demon of the underworld: it radiated hatred and projected malice. Its true form still contained in the curator's mortal form there was no denying its true identity shone through, from the blood red eyes to the sharpened claws that had broken through the nail beds of the mortals flesh.

"How did she manage to get away? I thought you were confident in fetching her for me."

The demon's voice dripped with hate, its scratchy sound grated against Apollos nerves.

"The warrior was aware of our presence. He was prepared and vanished as soon as we appeared."

Apollo glared, his own gaze hard, his power pulsed around him as he detected the lie but didn't confront the untruth. He huffed, much like a spoilt child, "So you are telling me that you," he pointed towards the demon as he paced. "You, one of the darkest creatures from the underworld, failed. Even with help from your pack of dogs," he continued to rant, "to apprehend one small mortal female with no battle skills and failed to kill off a simple mortal warrior?" Apollo continued to stomp his way across the stage, the eyes of the creatures and that of Devastation followed. "You are seriously making me rethink your usefulness, perhaps I should return you to your purgatory."

The demon growled in response and in turn caused the other creatures to bow their submission to him. As with all things, there was a hierarchy even within the depths of hell and Apollo had managed to drag up its king.

"So again I ask, why did you let her escape?"

Devastation smiled and revealed rows of sharp teeth and canine teeth that dripped with saliva. Dominance pulsed from its form. Apollo would have to step carefully if he wanted to retain control of this being. The last thing he needed was a rampage that would attract the attention of his fellow gods.

"The warrior is strong." Apollo's eyebrow raised as the demon spoke, the god folded his muscled arms across his chest and shrugged.

"So… Kill him."

The demon clenched its fists until its claws sliced into its palms and released a torrent of blood onto the wooden floor.

"he isn't mortal."

Apollo didn't react but for the widening of his eyes; he started to pace once again.

"So when has that mattered before? Separate them and grab her, it's as simple as that. No more excuses," Apollo ground out, his right hand lifted in the air. "Don't make me regret freeing you."

With a snap of his fingers the god disappeared in a flash of gold, leaving the demon and its creatures to finish their meal.

Chapter Twenty-Four

Sonia switched off the engine and looked out of the window towards the cottage. The weather was typical of the wonderful UK coastline — blustery with lots of cloud that flew by overhead and every now and again gave a glimpse of the sun trying to peak its rays out. The meadow that surrounded the small cottage ran until it hit the cliff edge and overlooked the Irish Sea. The tall grass and flowers swayed in perfect rhythm with the wind and rippled like that of a surface of a pond. It was beautifully calming and Sonia found herself mesmerised by the scene.

Memories of her simple yet happy childhood played like a movie through her mind. Her imagination easily saw them playing through the meadow and being chased by her mother as her father watched on a smile across his lips. There wasn't a day that went by that Sonia didn't miss them. After over twenty years of them being gone she still felt overwhelmed by the grief that could take hold. The details of that time had become hazy but the feeling of loss never lessened. She was thankful and blessed she still had her grandma who had taken over the role of guardian and raised her. For a young child dealing with grief, the hectic dreams, visions and constant headaches, she nearly toppled under the pressure. If not for the care of Rosa, Sonia was sure she would have been medicated and placed in a mental facility.

Grandma Rosa was the only one that could help her understand what was happening, she was the only one Sonia could rely on to make sense of the shit storm her life had become all of a sudden.

"Sonia," Cosmos' voice purred across her senses and pulled her out of her self-pity. She hadn't realised it but she had just been sat there staring into space. "Is all ok?" His voice settled her thoughts and managed to ground her, she nodded and attempted a smile.

"Yes, Cosmos, sorry I was miles away there. This is my grandma's home." Sonia frowned when no one appeared at the front door. "I thought she would be in."

Sonia removed the key from the ignition and tapped it on the steering wheel.

"Tis a wondrous place, mayhap she is enjoying the vista?"

Sonia smiled and shook her head, the way he always sounded so formal make her insides twist.

"I doubt she is home. She always had a knack of knowing when people would visit and she would always be there at the front door in greeting. Maybe she is out at the shops."

She climbed out of the car more than thankful to be out of the enclosed space, his whole being dominated and it made it hard to breathe and think. She watched as he unfolded himself from the passenger seat of the Mini. It made her chuckle watching a man as big as him try to get out without looking like a human pretzel. As much as his presence so far had been somewhat nerve wracking and brought feelings she had hidden deep down out, he made her feel safe. She also found comfort in the fact he was now taking at least some interest in her and not blaming her for their current situation. She didn't wait to approach the door, knowing he would follow her anyway, she tried the door handle. As she expected it was locked. That proved for once her grandma definitely wasn't at home and for the first time in, well, forever she hadn't been here to greet her. 'Strange,' Sonia thought. Rosa would always let her know if she would be out of town.

"Sonia?" His voice whispered across her ears and she hadn't even noticed that he was stood right behind her — his breath was warm on the back of her neck. His body heat radiated towards her and made her want to lean back into his strong embrace.

"She's not home," she admitted out loud. "I'm hoping she left me a key somewhere." She moved away from the warrior and headed around the side of the cottage. Her feet crunched upon the gravel as she walked around the old structure, past the flowering Clematis that had covered the West wall and through the small swinging gate that separated the wild meadow of the front from the slightly tidier picturesque back garden. Lavender bloomed in dozens of pots scattered in a haphazard pattern, the aroma filled her senses as she walked passed the raised planters that held vegetables and herbs and in the centre to all of this a simple wooden frame that held a large cushioned swing. Even more pots lined the back wall of the cottage filled to the brim with more flowers and a climbing rose that had swept around the back door as if it was its guardian. Sonia tried the back door and sighed as this too was locked. Now what would she do.

"Grandma, where the hell are you? I need you," Sonia grumbled out loud as she moved to peek into the kitchen window. She turned and watched as the wind picked up again and rippled through the flowers, the sun chose that moment to shine through the clouds, improving the dismal day instantly and it drew Sonia's gaze to the planter next to the door. A hint of gold twinkled in the brief sunlight and highlighted the location of a key. Grandma Rosa may not be there in person but yet again she proved her uncanny gift correct and guessed that Sonia would be visiting. Sonia grinned and picked up the key, she dusted off the soil from the planter and tried it in the door, with one turn the door unlocked and Sonia was able to step into the small kitchen.

"Thanks, Grandma," she breathed to herself, only to hear Cosmos answering chuckle from behind her.

"Do you talk to yourself often, hellcat?" His tone was teasing as he ducked under the door frame and stepped inside. Sonia shrugged but couldn't stop a smile from gracing her lips as she looked at the warrior that now filled the kitchen.

"Sometimes. It's an old habit."

She turned towards the rest of the cottage, only two other rooms and they were both tidy but empty. The smell of homemade brownies filled the small home and made Sonia's stomach growl. With an embarrassed flush she eyed Cosmos who seemed to be doing some exploring of his own, his head bent deep into the pantry. With a whoop of delight he pulled out a basket covered in a dish cloth but with an envelope attached to the side. Sonia's name was written clearly in Grandma Rosa's unique scribble.

"These are what we can smell, yes?" Cosmos placed the basket upon the kitchen table and moved the cloth away revealing the treats inside.

"Yes, they are and they taste so good. Help yourself," Sonia said as she grabbed the envelope and ripped into it.

Chapter Twenty-Five

"My lady, Oracle, it has been a long time."

Rosa, current oracle to the gods, sat comfortably on a sun lounger that was located on a terrace that circled a spectacular villa in Greece. Her guest none other than the great god Zeus himself sat relaxed in board shorts and a tight white t-shirt that showcased every muscle. Aviator sunglasses covered his eyes and his hair had been tied back. Rosa was unfazed by his beauty and smiled back, her hands in her lap as she waited for the god to stop with the pleasantries and get to the point. He was right, though, it had been a very long time since she had dealt with the gods directly. They usually sent Hermes to do their bidding and he was always the more pleasant one, Rosa smiled fondly. Hermes always made her smile and had helped her deal with the grief of losing Burt a few years back.

Rosa eyed the god in front of her, she knew time was of the essence for she had seen the coming battle that would bring the gods back into the mortal world; all because one of their own was a spoilt brat who wasn't getting things his own way. Reluctantly she had left her cottage with no word to her granddaughter, Sonia, about where she was and went straight to the old villa that had been in the family for generations. What Rosa regretted the most was lying to Sonia — the child had no idea who and what she was or that the coming battle was centred on her.

"Zeus, it has indeed been a long time."

The great god smiled and revealed straight white teeth and dimples that peaked out from his goatee.

"The years have been kind, Rosa. You are well?"

Rosa laughed. Zeus never changed; he was always the charmer.

"Ahh, the famous Zeus charm out in force. You must be desperate to use that little trick on me. Shall we cut to the chase? Why am I here and not training my granddaughter for what is coming?"

Zeus sighed and stood. He removed the glasses from his face and Rosa got her very first look at a seriously concerned god.

"I am sorry, Rosa, but you know the rules. We abide by balance as you know but to put it bluntly the balance is going to shit. The only way to stop things getting any worse is to try and stop Apollo. By removing you, the current Oracle, I have removed a secondary source for him to gain access to the creatures and demons of the underworld. I have no idea how he found you, Rosa, I have kept your bloodline a secret since the glory days and only Hermes knew you by face. Apollo must find your Sonia before time runs out and his precious portal is closed. I am hoping he runs out of time but you know full well he is stubborn."

"I understand but she has no idea who or what she is. How can you expect her to fight the sun god when she doesn't even believe in you all? She never did when I told her our history as a child." Rosa stood and stumbled towards the railing where the god looked out over the sea, her legs creaking in their old age. "Why is it none of you can play nice with each other? Why must you always involve us mortals?"

Zeus chuckled. "Perhaps it is because we were never born, just created by the will of the universe, so we have never been schooled as a child is by its parents."

"Well, some of you need a smack round the back of the legs," Rosa shook her head and touched the god's arm. " I have never requested anything from the gods, but I ask you to protect my Sonia."

Zeus took Rosa's hand in his own and lifted it to his lips, true affection for the old woman lay in his eyes.

"She is protected, Rosa, she has found her match. You know Aphrodite has become involved and when that women gets involved you know something special will happen." He smiled again before releasing her hand.

"Good, I may be old but I can still kick arse, I think that's how Sonia says it, and yes I know about the warrior. I am the Oracle after all and as such I have done my part to help Sonia." Rosa closed her eyes and felt for her power.

"I cannot see the ending, Zeus, only the beginning. She has a long way to go."

"I know, Rosa, we all have. The consequences of this will change Olympus for all time," he sighed before he placed his glasses back over his eyes and held his hand out again.

"Come, Oracle, let us dine and reminisce, I have need to forget the present time for a while."

Chapter Twenty-Six

Sonia, my princess,
I am sorry I am not home to meet you and your warrior (Yes, I know about him) Help yourself to the brownies, I made them for you. There is more food in the fridge should you need it.
Your room as always is ready.
There are so many things that I should have told you about what and who you are, but I will let your mother do that as is her right. Keep an open mind, my dear. Go to my room and on the top shelf of my cupboard is a shoe box with your name on it. That, my dear Sonia, is your legacy and know this, if we never meet again I will be waiting to see you in Elyssia.
I love you,
G-Rosa
Give the small note to your warrior, my dear, and make sure he doesn't eat all the brownies.

Sonia frowned and sat down hard on the chair at the kitchen table. Why was everyone always so damn cryptic? Frustrated, she slammed the note down upon the kitchen table and gasped in pain as she hit her injured hand.

"Fuck! Shit! Bollocks!"

"Hellcat, let me see."

Sonia again was shocked by how quick Cosmos had moved to her side. He gently cupped her injured hand within his own and slowly unravelled the bandages. Layer after layer came away, each one stained with more blood than the other. By the time he had completely taken it off a small pool of blood had collected in her palm.

"Shit, why is it still bleeding? Shouldn't it have stopped by now?" Sonia lifted her worried gaze to that of Cosmos, his eyes focused completely on her hand and his frown matched hers as he paced his other palm over the wound and closed his eyes. Sonia was completely entranced — with his eyes shut his face was serene but still devastatingly handsome. His lips were her sole focus and the harder she tried to look elsewhere the more they came back to them. She wondered what it would be like to kiss them, to be at their mercy as they took control. Sonia was so engrossed in her own little fantasy world she nearly missed the warmth that had started to travel up her arm from her palm. She flicked her eyes from her hand back up to Cosmos and gasped as his own opened to reveal his emerald green eyes, they sparkled with a gold light.

"Cosmos," she whispered. "What are you doing?"

"Trying to heal you," Cosmos' voice was deep and husky and Sonia was unable to tear her gaze from his. Her hand pulsed with heat and his eyes had turned almost golden. She leant forward as if being tugged, a mere breath separated them.

"But how?"

His voice seemed to get deeper and deeper as the heat built, "I know not how but I must."

Sonia was surprised with how much emotion was laced in his words. Like healing her hand meant more, almost as if she meant something to him. The heat stopped and she immediately missed the tingle it had created, a forced glance away from his eyes that had returned to their stunning green she watched as he removed his hand revealing a now healed palm with only a small red scar that bisected her palm. The pain that she had spent the last twenty-four hours feeling had vanished but in its place was a slow burn, a burn for this mysteriously alpha male that threw her off balance.

Surely it wasn't normal to have feelings like this so quickly after meeting someone. It couldn't be normal to feel like your whole world depended and revolved around this one person. Every time he touched her she lost her train of thought and when he really looked at her with those emerald eyes it felt like he saw through her to her soul. The thing is, those eyes of his, they felt like she was coming home and that was dangerous.

"Cosmos," his name fell from her lips a moment before she acted on her desire and pressed her own against his. She pressed softly at first, amazed at how soft they actually were. She must have taken him by surprise as he seemed to freeze, not moving a muscle, letting her explore. His lips parted slightly allowing Sonia's tongue to delve into its heat. A slight whimper of pleasure escaped as she took in his taste, chocolate mixed with spice, that was unique to only him.

As if her groan had pulled him from his daze Cosmos reacted in that instant, his hands thrusted into her hair and held her still whilst he took over the kiss, branding her with his essence as he thrusted his tongue into the deep recesses of her mouth, mimicking his obvious intent with what he wanted to do to the rest of her body. He kept one hand in her hair and the other slid slowly down her body. His fingertips caressed her side, past her breast until they slid around her waist. With no effort he had her on his lap without even breaking the kiss that was destroying every memory she had of being kissed by another man. This was it for Sonia, this was the kiss and quite possibly the man, that ruined her for all future men.

Sonia's hands clutched at his chest as she rode out the storm that was his kiss. Her body unconsciously rubbed against his in a bid to get closer. She was almost mindless until sanity slowly returned and she forced herself away. Her breaths ragged, Sonia unclenched her fingers from his sweater and faced him. His eyes blazed with lust, his own chest heaved as he rubbed a hand up her back and moved the other from her hair to her cheek.

"You are so damn beautiful."

Sonia blushed and tilted her head away, embarrassed that she had thrown herself at him and also scared of the intense look he was throwing her way.

"Thank you for healing me, Cosmos," she whispered, she still didn't trust her voice. She felt him sweep a lock of hair behind her ear as he answered

"It was my pleasure, Sonia. I wish I could have don't it sooner." He took her palm into his hand and brought it to his lips. His eyes locked with hers as he kissed the centre right over the newly formed scar. His eyes claimed her just as the kiss had and for once Sonia wanted to embrace the feeling of belonging to someone and not just as someone's trophy. He tightened his hold on her and brought his mouth to her ear.

"I would do a lot more than heal you, Sonia, if you would let me." He kissed the skin just behind her ear, "I want the vision." He sat back in the chair and let Sonia slide off his lap, a small smirk tilted his lips and he grabbed another brownie as well as the note left for him by her grandma and stood. "I will be outside should you need me, Sonia."

Sonia's mouth opened and closed. What the hell? Her face blushed bright red as she remembered the vision he was talking about. How did he know about that? She turned and hid her face, scared that he would see her own look of desire at the thought of what had happened. As she peeked over her shoulder he had already walked out of the kitchen leaving her alone to deal with the next step in finding out what the hell was going on. That man had her in knots but right now she had her legacy to find.

Grandma Rosa' bedroom was small but cosy. Her double bed sat underneath the window covered by the generic patchwork quilt. Her bedside table held a small lamp, a wind up clock and two picture frames — one with a black and white picture of Grandma and Grandpa Burt taken on a beach somewhere. Their faces shone with happiness. The other was of Sonia's mum and dad with a very small Sonia in their arms. Bright beaming smiles shone out at her from the frames and made Sonia's heart hurt with longing. She missed them so much it almost brought her to tears.

Fighting the need to sob, Sonia walked over to the inbuilt cupboard. Rosa's clothes hung neatly and her shoes were stacked against the back wall. She smiled and couldn't resist smelling one of Rosa's cardigans that hung closest to her. The scent of lavender clung to the cloth and reminded her of nights sat in her lap as she told stories to help get her to sleep. Sonia looked up onto the top shelf and spotted the brown shoe box, her name written in a swirling font on the side, and caught her eye. On tip toes Sonia reached up and snagged the box. A thick coating of dust coated the lid, she tried not to sneeze as she walked with it back to Grandma's bed and sat down, nerves had all of a sudden taken root within her stomach and she felt slightly nauseous.

A deep breath in and then out before Sonia removed the lid and emptied the contents out onto the quilt. A thick cream envelope fell out first followed by a solid silver coloured photo frame that held a picture of her mum and dad on their wedding day along with other pictures that were loose. Also a pair of cufflinks with a beautiful blue stone set into a silver bar, nestled next to it was a small velvet drawstring bag. A quick tug and she had it undone — the contents emptied into her palm.

Sonia had to hold back a sob as she looked down at the treasure. A long silver chain that held a blue topaz pendant over an inch squared in size. The stone shimmered and sparkled in the sun that shone through the window. Sonia remembered her mother wearing this. She remembered as a child she used to tug on the deceptively sturdy chain and chew on it. Tears slowly trickled down her cheeks as she drew the chain over her head and let the pendant settle down her cleavage. The chain was a bit long for Sonia's liking but it felt right just where it was.

Finally, Sonia eyed the envelope, her name neatly penned on the front. She was unable to hold back the tears as they slid down her face. This was her mum's handwriting, her mum had held this envelope in her hand. Unable to wait any longer Sonia ripped into the paper, her fingers shook as she pulled out the thick cream paper covered in more of her mum's beautiful script. With another deep breath and a wipe of her eyes she unfolded the letter.

My Darling Daughter Sonia,
If you are reading this then I am not around to see you grow into the beautiful, confident woman I always knew you would be. Deep down I always knew we would never get to see you grow, marry and have children of your own. I was always convinced I would have more time.
I wish with all my heart I could have told you all of this to your face, my darling, and not just words on a page.
Please never forget that I love you but you need to know who and what you are. I'm just sorry I kept this from you for so long.
Remember those stories Grandma used to tell you to get you to sleep?
The ones about those special ladies and the gods.
Well, they are not stories, Sonia, they are our family's history, our legacy so to speak.
Can you remember what those ladies were called?

Sonia breathed in and out as she read the words. Those stories had always sounded so farfetched and out of this world that she never would have believed them and she still didn't. She thought back to the last time her grandma had sat her down for story time. One word stuck out more than others, Sonia spoke out loud.

"Oracles. They were called Oracles."

I know you know what I am talking about, my dear, you were never stupid. Sonia, my darling, you are an Oracle, descended from a long line of women that were handpicked by the gods.

Don't sit and read this, Sonia, and think I am talking rubbish. You always did laugh at the stories and put them down to the very overactive imagination of your grandma. But believe me they are true. Search deep down inside yourself and you will feel I am right.

Those dreams, Sonia, as well as the headaches you have been having, they are your powers trying to come through. They want to be used. It's in your blood.

As Oracles, Sonia, we are allowed glimpses into a future yet to come. Although that path has been started the destination is yet to be set. With our help people's lives and their fates could be changed and this is why we have always been protected and revered. Over time, Sonia, as you know, the people's beliefs changed and the worship of the gods ground to a halt. Their beliefs in the oracles too vanished and as such we were no longer wanted or needed by the mortals.

That left us vulnerable and open to attacks and not just of the battle kind. Never forget you come from a line of beautiful alluring women and as such as soon as the mortals believed we were no longer protected they decided to take what they saw as free game.

So we vanished. Even from most of the gods. Only a few knew that we had survived.

Sonia, I know right now you are confused and I'm sorry. More sorry than I ever thought. I made a choice when you were born and I don't regret it because it meant even though I'm not there in person I can still help you in some way.

I chose to see your future at the cost of my own. Sonia, the gods are real, as real as you or your grandma.

They will always demand balance and as an Oracle that is what you are able to provide them. A glimpse as to how they can keep that balance.

In my vision of your future I saw the fight you will become involved in but I didn't see the outcome, but I hope my next words will help settle any doubts that plague you.

As a gift from the gods for our service we were each gifted a guarantee of protection. A promise that there would be one soul meant for us. That one soul that once found would protect and cherish our hearts and would, in the god's stead, protect our bodies.

A predestined mate made for you and you alone. Your father was mine and I know deep within my heart that you would have met yours by the time you read this. I know the feelings are confusing you and you think it is all too sudden but believe me when I say he is your match in every way and he will protect you with his life. He is unlike any other man and will love you like no other. Sonia, he is your soulmate.

Trust in your warrior, my darling girl, for your souls are meant to be together and you are stronger together than apart.

Believe in yourself.

You are so much stronger than you think you are.

We will see each other again, my darling.

But not yet,

Momma

Xx

Sobs wracked Sonia's whole body as she let the letter fall from her fingers and onto the floor. She was torn between rereading the letter to try to absorb her mother's warmth and love and ripping the letter to shreds and denying everything that was written. She didn't think she had the strength to accept what had been said. She wasn't as strong as her mum had mentioned and the very idea that gods were real as well as her being some sort of future telling Oracle. She didn't need that sort of pressure and it made her want to curl up in a ball in the corner of the room and hide away from the world. With neither her mother nor Rosa around to help her deal with the information all she could do was sob, sob until her chest hurt, her eyes stung and her voice had become hoarse. Her mind felt total confusion but as it slowly processed every tiny detail it all started to click into place. What had happened to Arianna made more sense. Who Arcaeus, or Matthew, and Cosmos really were and even the involvement of the gods started to feel more believable. Being called an Oracle actually felt right and in her heart, as her mother had said, he made sense of all the dreams and visions she had been having. She realised she had already seen part of her future and it didn't look as promising as her mother had made out. She remembered the feeling of being lifted with a hand to her throat as her breath was choked out of her by a male with golden hair. And then there was Cosmos, the letter explained why she had such intense feelings for him so soon after meeting him and why whenever she was around him she felt a sense of safety. With any other man Sonia had been confident and in charge, yet with Cosmos she was happy to let him take control. No other man had pulled at her heart and that said in itself that she had already fallen for him. Sonia thought back and knew she had fallen for him the moment she had seen his image within the mosaic, her mind was just slower to catch on.

Sonia took the pendant within her fingers and looked deep into the blue stone. She brought it to her lips and kissed it before she dropped it back to rest against her chest. Regardless of her future she needed to start living for her and not what everyone expected of her and with regards to men it was time she followed her heart. There was a man downstairs that had shown her true passion and she would be damned if she'd let that flit away. Maybe it was about time she just let someone else take control. She just hoped she was making the right decision.

Chapter Twenty-Seven

Cosmos sat on the cushioned swing in the back garden and watched the cottage for any sign of Sonia. He had been sneaky when he had read the letter from her grandma over her shoulder but he couldn't help it. He would do whatever it took to help protect her and whatever information she was currently being given would affect his ability to do that. As she had gone upstairs to find whatever it was she had been left he had gone out to the metal beast and retrieved the bags from within. His ego was still a little bruised from the fact it had taken him over half an hour to just get inside that thing. He had also retrieved his swords and would have them close at all times. He had an unnerving feeling that he would require them sooner rather than later.

When he had taken the bags inside he had heard Sonia's quiet sobs but knew his company would not be wanted should he go to find her, even though every being in his body called for him to take her in his arms and make her smile instead of cry. He thought back to the kiss and his body responded instantly. She had lived up to her nickname of hellcat and Cosmos was more than willing for more of that. He not only wanted to protect her but she called at every instinct he had that wanted to possess her, brand her with himself so that she and every other male would know who she really belonged to.

He clutched at the note he had been left. It hadn't surprised him in the slightest that her grandmother had been aware of him but the contents made him nervous, made him realise how much he needed Sonia and for her to need him in return. He smiled at the advice in the letter — it made him feel like he had an ally in his bid to make Sonia his. Cosmos looked down and reread it for the third time.

Warrior,
Welcome to the modern world, I hope you are settling in well.
First off I should tell you who and what Sonia is. She is the last Oracle to have been born. She knows nothing of the extent of her gift and she doesn't realise how much danger she is in.
I would be there but as you know when the gods call, you answer.
Now, you need to know that modern women are nothing like those wenches you were used to back in your time. So here is a little advice for I know you will need it.
Don't say things you think she wants to hear, my Sonia prefers people to be up front and say it how it is. Plus, she's a bugger at knowing if you are lying.
Don't lie to her, she will hurt you back. Usually with a kick to the nuts (just being honest, I want great grandbabies one day)
Treat her with the respect she deserves.
You know as an Oracle she will require your protection and the gods did deem you worthy enough to send you to her so don't balls it up. Protect her and love her, Warrior, for she was made for you.
Every Oracle has their one and you, my dear, are it for Sonia.
Trust your instincts.

Cosmos pushed himself back and forth on the swing as he folded the letter up and placed it in the front pocket of his jeans. He wiggled in the seat a little — he was still getting used to wearing these strange garments — they were comfortable, though, and he no longer had that annoying draft that always seemed to waft up his kilt.

Cosmos was so deep in thought that he missed Sonia as she called out his name. It wasn't until she stood just in front of him, her eyes held a deep sadness that called to him, but also beneath there lay a fight that he knew would take over and prove what a strong and intelligent woman she was. Oracle or not, fate or not, he would protect and love her.

"Cosmos, are you ok? I was calling you."

He smiled and reached up to hold her hand. Her skin was soft under his fingers as he tugged her forward. He stopped his swing on the chair and pulled her in between his knees. Cosmos took his time looking at her face, memorising every freckle. She still looked tired and slightly pale but she would always be beautiful to him.

"I apologise. I was deep in thought." He reached up to cup her cheek within his palm — still surprised when she leaned in to his touch and didn't back away. "Why have you been crying, hellcat?" He used her nickname to try and urge a smile from her lips as he slid his hands down to her waist and pulled her even closer to him. She still didn't answer but she looked as though she too was now deep in thought.

"Talk to me, Sonia. Tell me so I can help you." Cosmos didn't release her gaze and remembered the words within the letter about being upfront. With a deep breath he did what he had never done with anyone. He told her how he felt.

"Talk to me, my Oracle," her eyes widened as he stated he knew what she was. "I am here to protect you, but most of all I am here to love you. The gods created me and sent me to you, I am yours whether you desire it or not." He took one of her hands and placed it over his pec and right over his heart. "My heart is yours, little one, I think it has been since the first moment I saw you, maybe even before then when you were just a feeling I could sense whilst trapped. I have never felt like I belong anywhere, Sonia, always an outcast. Until you. I will live and die to make you happy." His words not only shocked Sonia but shocked himself, they had been from the heart as he let a side of himself out that he had hidden deep. He then realised that to love was never a weakness, it made him feel stronger. He watched as Sonia's eyes filled once again with tears and it tore at his heart.

"Sonia, please do not cry. It hurts to see you so upset." He lifted his hand from holding her hand to his chest and wiped away the tears with his thumb. "Say something, Sonia. A warrior can't unleash his soul like that and get not an answer from you."

Her voice was just a whisper as she circled her fingers on his chest, "You know what I am, you know that I have no idea what I am doing and that I am being hunted?" She didn't look into his eyes as she said this but instead watched her own fingers.

"Yes, Sonia" He kept his reply short as he wanted to hear her own words, desperate for what she would say.

"You make me feel nervous." Cosmos frowned: this wasn't what he was hoping to hear.

"I am sorry, hellcat." He didn't know what else to say to that but just sat and waited.

"You are the only man I have ever met that makes me nervous, Cosmos." She then looked into his eyes and, beneath the tears, they sparkled with more than just nerves. Was that affection?

"What are you saying, Sonia?"

Sonia than smiled shyly before she leant forward and gently pressed her lips to his, then she pulled back.

"What I am saying, Cosmos, is that… Well, I think… No, wait, I know that I love you."

Cosmos was stunned and his heart had started to beat so hard he felt like it was about to burst from within his chest. He slid both his arms around Sonia's waist and tugged her onto his lap, he lifted one hand and moved a lock of hair to behind her ear.

"That's good because I love you, my Oracle."

He sealed his lips over hers and took control, basking in the feeling of being loved and of Sonia clutching his shoulders. Her next words brought a growl from his mouth and had him storming towards the cottage.

"Make me forget, Cosmos. I just want to feel you… love me please."

Chapter Twenty-Eight

Sonia felt dazed as Cosmos practically marched them into the cottage. She couldn't fight the smile that had crept onto her lips as he seemed desperate to get them inside and where no one could see them. Not that she could blame him, she was more than keen to finally see him naked. Being teased with glimpses of his muscles when he had been wearing his warrior clothes had made Sonia just as desperate to get her hands on his bare skin.

As they entered the kitchen Sonia had to stifle a giggle with her hand over her mouth as Cosmos had stalled, not sure which way to go to get to the bedrooms. Her giggle died instantly within her throat as he looked from the kitchen table towards her and back again, she shook her head and smiled.

"Oh, hell no, warrior. That's not happening."

He grinned back at her, showcasing off his gorgeous lips and dimples as he turned and tugged her once again into his arms, his hands instantly going around her waist and down to the curve of her arse.

"Are you sure Hellcat?" he whispered against her ear. "There would be nothing more erotic than seeing you bent over that table waiting for me."

Sonia knew she was blushing. She bit her lip hard to stop a groan from escaping as his words created images inside her head.

"Or would you prefer to have me at your mercy, Sonia?" he continued as Sonia's heart rate started to rise. "You want me laid out for your pleasure as you straddle me and take what you need."

This time Sonia let the moan escape and she lay her head upon his shoulder in an attempt to hide her bright red cheeks, she let her own hands roam up and down his back. The images he had managed to create in her mind had heat building up from deep inside her. Her body burned for Cosmos' touch but as she had said she would not do that here at her grandma's kitchen table. Sonia forced herself to take a step back away from the heat of his body but she retained a hold of his hand and with a shy smile she led Cosmos through the kitchen and towards the stairs that led to the two small bedrooms. She didn't know why because it wasn't as if Cosmos was her first, but she wanted this to be done properly and not just a quick one time fumble. As usual Sonia wanted control but she knew the warrior trailing behind wouldn't give it up easily.

Her heavy breathing filled the air as they climbed the stairs and entered her old bedroom. A small double bed sat to the left, the wooden headboard worn with age and the duvet was another of Grandma Rosa's famous patchworks. Across from this was a simple chest dresser that held a small amount of her clothing for when she visited. There was no decoration as she had removed nearly everything when she had moved to the city.

Sonia turned as she heard Cosmos close the old fashioned latch door, she wasn't worried about the lack of the lack of a lock as they were the only ones in the cottage. Sonia was scared not of his desires but of her own. She had been with plenty of men and some might have said that she was a bit of a tart, but she had always managed to remain emotionally unattached, until now. Cosmos had managed in only a few days what she had stopped all other men from doing in years. The walls that she had erected around her heart after her first failed relationship had come clattering down. She knew now why those dates and relationships had never worked out was because her heart and soul had been waiting for Cosmos. Admitting that to herself she felt a weight lift from her shoulders almost like she had been bogged down with it for far too long. The relief was instantaneous.

Sonia lifted her chin to face the warrior and as their eyes connected, blue versus green, she felt like a swarm of butterflies had taken flight from inside her. Her eyes never left his as he stepped forward and lifted his hands to cup her cheek before he bent his head to hers. His lips were soft and the kiss was slow and tender, they stroked against hers urging them to part. His gentle assault had started the burn but it would quickly turn into an inferno. She loved the feel of his lips but Sonia needed more.

Sonia moved her hands down towards the hem of Cosmos' sweater; she tugged and then broke the kiss so she could tug it over his head in one movement. Sonia almost purred in delight to finally see his chest. Huge shoulders and flexing pecs got her adoration first, before her gaze travelled down over his solid abs. Each muscle defined and jumped when she reached out to touch him with her fingertips. His jeans hung low on his hips, showcasing that ridge of muscle that always made Sonia go weak at the knees. Sonia's eyes refused to stop roaming up and down his body, taking in a new detail with every sweep. A light dusting of hair covered his pecs — it was the lightest golden blonde and it continued its trail down his abs and under the waist band of his jeans.

Before Sonia was able to get her hands on the belt to his jeans, Cosmos took hold of her wrists and pushed them behind her back, locking her chest against his. Sonia closed her eyes as he started gentle kisses behind her ears and continued his trail down to her neck. Her body melted against his as the kisses became more and more dominant. Cosmos bit and licked her neck as he ground his arousal against her belly. He gently forced her back to arch as he placed his knee in between her thighs, his own rubbed her in the most delicious way and fuelled the fire that was burning her from the inside out.

"Oh god, Cosmos," her words were a breathy whisper and he held her body still taking his fill of her.

"Hellcat, you have far too much clothing on," he chuckled as she whimpered from the loss of his mouth on her own. He released her wrists and stood up, back upright, before he stepped back.

"Undress for me, Sonia," his words grumbled out and called to her as a plea and Sonia was helpless to refuse. She drew her hands slowly down over her body before she took the hem of her t-shirt in her hands and pulled it up and over her head. Her eyes still on Cosmos she dropped it to the floor and moved her hands to the button and fly on her jeans. With a kick of her feet she had freed her feet from her pumps and she wiggled the jeans down her legs and off. She was nervous as she stood there in her plain black bra and panties. She had never worried in the past about how she looked naked but now she wanted Cosmos to like what he saw. His eyes visibly widened as he looked his fill and Sonia fought the need to fidget. Cosmos had already undone the top button of his jeans and watched her intently with eyes that missed nothing. In the depths of the emerald green was again the swirling gold, it pulsed almost in time to Sonia's heartbeat. It pounded hard in her chest as they stood in silence and looked at each other — the tension made is hard to breathe.

Sonia swiped her tongue across her lips and the movement broke whatever spell had kept the warrior in place. In one stride he was in front of her, his hands swept around her waist and grasped her by her arse, he lifted her off the floor as he moved across the room to the bed. All the while his lips took possession of her own once again. His touch and kiss gave her no doubt that he desired her. His teeth again nipped at her skin as his hands roamed everywhere. Her underwear lasted only a few seconds as he growled and ripped them away from her body, showing, indeed, his strength. Sonia was lost to the pleasure and was unable to stop her own hands from wandering and touching every inch of his skin. Each and every time he bit into her sensitive skin her body convulsed and her core tightened as if there were a direct link. Sonia felt frantic as the ache in her core intensified. The feel of the buttons on his jeans as they pressed against her felt so good but it wasn't enough. Sonia used her nails to score down Cosmos' back as she arched into him, her breasts pressed flush against his chest. Her nipples pebbled, the tips were sensitive and called for some sort of attention.

"Hellcat," he breathed and placed an open mouthed kiss upon her neck as he grabbed her wrists and held them down by her sides. "Hold still or I will lose the small amount of control I have left."

Sonia could only nod as he started his trail of kisses down towards her breasts, finally giving them the attention they craved. He took a nipple into his hot mouth and sucked hard, making it hard before he used his teeth to gently tug. The fire that shot from her breast to her core had her arching off the bed and a moan falling from her lips. Sonia thrashed her head from side to side as she tried to breathe through the pleasurable assault. Her nipples had always been her weakness and Cosmos had found it and was using that and her body against her. She was so close to combustion just from his attention to her nipples she ignored his growl of warning, lifted her hands and thrust them into his hair. Her nails once again came into play as they scraped his scalp and she held him close to her chest — a silent plea for him to continue.

Sonia whimpered again as Cosmos pulled himself up and away from her clutching hands and backed off the bed. His look was one of pure lust as he stood and looked at her body spread out. His eyes locked with hers as he undid the final few buttons on his jeans. The thick material dropped to the floor with a thud and revealed him fully to her. She was already fully aware that he had refused to wear any sort of underwear but as he stood in front of her now, his hand wrapped around his thick cock, she nearly erupted then and there.

Standing tall and proud from a thatch of golden curls his cock stood ready. A bead of pre-cum glistened from the slit and called out to her to taste and lick it clean. His balls were drawn up tight and his thick thighs flexed as he again swept his palm up and down the thick shaft. Sonia licked her lips again unable to take her eyes away from the sight.

Cosmos' muscled legs bunched and flexed as he moved. He bent at the waist and collected her t-shirt from the floor. Showing his strength once again he ripped the material into strips. Sonia forgot to breathe as he climbed back onto the bed and prowled up her body. Just as he had done before, he placed tiny kisses onto her skin, along her belly and onto her chest, keeping them light and her on edge. His large callused palms took her wrists and forced her arms above her head.

"Sonia," his words were forced and harsh and he leant over her body and tied Sonia's wrists together and then in turn tied them to the bed frame.

"Cosmos?" Sonia tugged on the ties and pulled as she looked up at Cosmos, confusion etched upon her face. "What's going on?" She tugged again in a futile attempt to get free.

"Shhh!" Cosmos stroked her face and kissed her lips. "Hellcat, relax, I want you to close your eyes and just let go." His breath tingled on her neck as his hand restarted their journey down her body lightly touching her skin as he moved his lips back to her own. "Trust in me that I won't hurt you." He sucked on her bottom lip, "But if you keep scratching me with those kitten claws I won't last long enough to make you scream my name like I want to."

His hands moved again to her breast, he tweaked her nipple and he pushed the hard ridge of his cock against her wet core. "Feel that, Sonia," he said as he bucked his hips against hers, his cock pushed on her clit and brought a groan from her mouth.

"That's what you have done to me, hellcat, but first I want to see you give up control to me." He moved his lips back to Sonia's and sealed against them in a brutal kiss, one that robbed her of breath and stoked the fire even higher. "Do you trust me?" he breathed, his eyes searched her gaze. Sonia knew in that moment that she trusted him as she had no other. She trusted him with her life and body. She was on fire for his touch and she whispered her answer as she wrapped her legs high around his waist and pushed her body against his.

"I trust you, Cosmos."

Lifting her head Sonia pressed her lips against his, giving up any and all control to him. They both groaned as Cosmos' own control slipped. His hands and lips were suddenly everywhere and once again brought Sonia's body back up to boiling point. Sonia was positive she couldn't take much more at the same time she wanted it to go on for ever. His hands had moved lower and she felt his fingers gently tease her core. He groaned as he parted her lips and found her soaked slit.

"Fuck, Sonia, you are so wet."

Gently at first he buried one finger inside her, her hips thrust in response, it felt amazing but Sonia wanted more. She was hung over the edge and she couldn't help but beg.

"Cosmos, please," she whimpered his name and then cried out as he slid a second finger to join the first and his eyes watched her reactions.

Chapter Twenty-Nine

Cosmos was going to explode if he didn't either calm the hell down or get her ready enough to receive him. He wasn't a small man and she felt so damn tight as she clenched around his fingers he dreaded hurting her. In all honesty when she had stripped down to her skimpy undergarments he had nearly lost it then and there. If it hadn't have been for his warrior training he was sure he would have lost it like a youth with his first wench. He had never met anyone who was as responsive to his touch like his hellcat and that didn't help his current issue. He was strung tight like a bow so when she had started to use her nails on him he had been close to bowing under the pressure. Now he had her tied to the bed and spread out she looked like a sacrifice that lay waiting. Waiting for him to bring her the most pleasure she had ever felt. He knew this time would be a quick coupling but that would only be the start. "You feel so damn good, hellcat, are you sure you are ready for me?"

Cosmos watched in pleasure as Sonia thrashed her head from side to side on the pillow, her body arching under the assault of his hands. He increased his pace with his fingers, scissoring them and twisting until he hit those secret buttons of nerves that had her panting, at the same time he pinched her clit hard. His reward was instant, her back again arched off the bed and his name fell from her lips in a strangled cry at the same moment her soaking core clenched down hard upon his fingers. Cosmos grinned, the sight of Sonia in the throes of pleasure only increased the ache in his balls. He leant back on to his heels and he removed his finger gently from her core, sweeping some of her nectar into his palm he used it to coat his thick cock. His palm engulfed the length and he groaned as he pumped once then twice. The friction felt so good but not nearly as good as what he knew she would feel like.

Sonia's eyes glazed as she watched his hand just before he leant forward once again and rubbed the head of his cock against her dripping entrance.

"Are you ready, Sonia?" His deep voice filled the room and called to her. Cosmos clenched his jaw as he placed himself at her entrance and slowly pushed.

"Ahh, fuck," he groaned as her pussy accepted him. He felt it clamp down on him and it also pulsed with the tiny aftershocks of her recent orgasm. Sweat beaded on his brow as he kept the thrust shallow and he pushed deeper until he was all the way in and his balls nestled against her arse.

"Oh, god. Fuck, Cosmos, you feel so good… Oh, god." Her incoherent cries of passion filled Cosmos with pride and encouraged him to thrust slow and deep. His hands had moved to her hips and lifted so he could slide inside even deeper.

"Sonia!" he called out as he once again lost control, letting his hips piston in and out as his fingers dug into her skin. A snarl erupted from his lips as he continued to pound deep inside Sonia's body. He watched again as she cried out — her body arching into his as her hands tugged on the ties that held her arms above her head. She exploded around him a moment later, her body tightening on his like a vice and forced a climax to erupt from his body. Cosmos tilted his head back and growled out his own cry of pleasure, the veins in his neck pulsed and his muscle bulged. He almost collapsed down onto an equally spent Sonia. He had seen stars the moment his body had spent his seed deep within her own — it was either the stars or passing out, and his pride would not have let that happen. In all his life he had never had a release that had been that intense, but as he looked down upon Sonia's face he knew why. No other had claimed his heart or his soul like she had done. What they had wasn't merely just sex but a connection that bonded them together.

Cosmos smiled and swept her hair from her face as she opened her eyes to look up at him, trust and love in her eyes.

"Wow," she whispered and nuzzled his palm.

"Wow indeed, my love." Cosmos finally allowed himself to use that endearment, he had wanted to use it all day. He leant in and whispered back, "But that was just the start, my hellcat."

Her eyes widened and then she grinned back as he had begun to grow hard once again, his shallow thrusts sending tingles up his spine and brought more groans from Sonia's lips. He reached over with one hand and removed the ties from her wrists, bringing one at a time to kiss the slight marks there. In Cosmos' mind he didn't think he would ever get enough of her.

Chapter Thirty

Meton watched his goddess with sad eyes. She hadn't regained consciousness in over three hours and he was worried he would never get to see her beautiful violet eyes shining back at him.

The goddess of love lay on her raised bed, her skin now as pale as snow and her chest barely moved. Her immortal glow had vanished and now Meton felt completely helpless. Whatever Apollo had done it was slowly killing her, draining her powers and her very essence with it. All so he could fuel his insane plans of domination and without Love herself the mortal world would suffer. Each god was tied to that realm regardless of their current belief system. It was simple, if love died it would become almost none existent in the world. Love was hard enough to find for the mortals but without Aphrodite giving it that nudge it would vanish all together. This would happen if any of the other deities were to fall. Meton shook his wings and stretched before he tucked them again back into his sides, then tilted his head to watch as the god of the underworld returned.

"My lord, is there any news?" Hades shook his head and folded his meaty arms across his chest. Gone were his robes that usually gave him a dark aura and instead he stood in a pair of black jeans and a plain black t-shirt. If it wasn't for his size he would easily pass as a mortal except his eyes gave him away.

"No, Meton, not yet. Zeus has gone to the mortal world to collect the current Oracle in the hopes of stopping Apollo that way, but that is all he is willing to do. It is up to the warrior, Cosmos, to protect the next Oracle and stop Apollo from freeing the creatures."

Meton nodded in return. The elder gods were forbidden to get involved unless the issue directly affected them. It was one of the many rules brought in to affect to give the other gods a sense of relief that they wouldn't abuse their powers.

"I understand, my lord. Is there anything we can do for my goddess?"

Hades walked over to stand by the great golden eagle, they both watched the rise and fall of her chest, afraid each one would be her last.

"I'm sorry, Meton, I cannot wake her. Whatever Apollo has done to her is draining her quickly and I'm afraid that if I use my powers then they could get tied in and he could very well start draining mine along with hers.

Meton's feathered head bowed, "What about her protection charms, will they still be affective?"

Hades' eyes narrowed before he shook his head, "No, they would have vanished as soon as the goddess lost consciousness this last time."

Meton's feathers ruffled and he shifted upon his perch and he never once took his eyes from Aphrodite.

"Then Aphrodite's charges will have been left unprotected, especially Arianna and Arcaeus."

Hades' frown continued before he nodded a final time.

"Ok worry not, Meton. I will go myself and check on them, I will also do what I can to assist. My worry, though, is that I am already too late to help the warrior."

Meton bowed low as he finally took his eyes away from the bed.

"Anything you need, my lord, I am here."

"Stay with your goddess, Meton. If I have need of you I will call. Pray that we can sort this mess out or Olympus may never be the same."

"Yes, my lord" Meton settled back onto his perch. Hades looked from the great golden bird to the still form of the goddess and for once he could see clearly what he had missed before. It wasn't the love of the mortals keeping the goddess with them it was the love from a single soul, a soul that would give everything he had to keep her safe.

Chapter Thirty-One

Sonia opened her eyes as she greeted the early morning sun. In their haste for each other they had forgotten about the curtains and in the bed, hidden from the world, Sonia had never felt happier. She felt cocooned in the arms of Cosmos as he lay spooned up behind her, his arm was thrown over her waist and held her tight, his hand cupped possessively over her stomach. His thick thigh was wedged between her own, instead of having to fight a wave of rising panic like she had in the past she felt safe and at peace. Usually after a night of hot sex she would have been out of the door before they had woken, but now she was more than happy to stay and enjoy the afterglow.

Her body, although tender from the attention of her warrior, hummed with pleasure and a silly smile crossed her lips as she thought of all the naughty things they had done to one another. Cosmos had been completely dominant over her body, taking her to heights she had never been to before. She knew she had bruises from his tight grip and she didn't care. They were a way to prove how much he had wanted her and how he had lost control.

Cosmos was still sound asleep so Sonia was able to slide out of his arms and out of bed. She was then able to stand there and look down at the warrior and how he had taken over the bed. He lay still on his side, his hand that had been clutched at her waist now lay where she had been. His face was relaxed in sleep and he had an innocent boyish edge to his features. There was a days worth of stubble across his chin and she could now see a faint scar that ran from his chin up his cheek and into his hairline.

Sonia walked over to her dresser and pulled out a set of shorts and a plaint t-shirt, she chuckled as she looked at the tattered remains of her t-shirt from the night before. The strips were strewn about and the memory of them made her shiver. Sonia tiptoed out of the room and headed downstairs to the kitchen. She would make them some breakfast and hopefully they would get to spend some more time together. Sonia had certainly drummed up and appetite and she didn't doubt that Cosmos could put away his body weight in food.

Sonia had dressed quickly, forgoing panties and a bra, she didn't see the point if they were going to continue what they had been doing last night. Once in the kitchen Sonia started to get everything ready as her mind drifted. So much had happened in such a short space of time, first the mosaic and then the appearance of the creatures and Cosmos. She had no idea what would happen now. How do you defeat creatures like that? Would she have to act like an Oracle and contact the gods? How would she do that if she needed to? These were all questions she needed answers for.

Sonia pulled cheese and eggs from the fridge and placed them on the table before getting the rest of the ingredients for a Spanish omelette. Sonia rarely cooked. She grinned at the thought of the hot-as-hell man upstairs in the bedroom — he was bloody worth it. Sonia again had no idea what would be in the future with them. She hoped things would work out and that she could figure out this whole Oracle business and with her grandma going AWOL she had no one to really turn to for answers. With a shake of her head Sonia moved her thoughts back to the warrior. How had he become so entrenched in her heart so quickly had to be a work of fate, and after what she had witnesses between Arianna and Arcaeus she was no longer going to question it. Sonia started to hum under her breath as she pottered about the kitchen, she barely even jumped when a pair of muscled arms circled her waist and pulled her back against an equally muscled body. A soft pair of lips started to nibble behind her ear and caused goosebumps to break out on her skin.

"Hellcat, next time you leave our bed without my knowing I'm tying you to it." His deep voice caressed her ear, "I did not enjoy waking up without you next to me."

Sonia could tell he was pouting in a manly way as he continued to nibble down behind her ear to her neck. She struggled to answer without sounding breathless.

"I wanted to make you breakfast," Sonia giggled as he squeezed her waist and she found she was disappointed that he had put his jeans back on.

"I figured you would be hungry and we need to keep your strength up," she laughed and turned in his arms, her hands rested on his chest. She felt him puff it up in response to her comment.

"I am strong, Sonia. Doubt me not on that."

Sonia leant up and kissed him quickly on the lips.

"I know you are strong, but I need to make sure you are able to keep up," Sonia smirked as she slid her hand down between them and cupped his growing arousal. His groan in response pleased Sonia, there was nothing sexier than hearing a man groan in pleasure and knowing she was the cause.

"Gods, hellcat, you keep that up and we won't get breakfast."

Sonia again grinned, patted his arousal gently and turned to continue cooking. Sonia was hot and needy again just from hearing him groan but she managed to hold herself back. She felt his warm breath again on her neck as well as his hard length press into her arse.

"You are a tease," he began as his hands teased her waist. "How would you feel if I tied your hands together, bent you over the table and fucked you until you begged me to stop?"

Sonia's hands had stopped stirring as her imagination ran away with his words, the ache had intensified and she had to clench her thighs to attempt to get some sort of relief. His voice held a husky edge as he continued.

"Thing is Sonia I wouldn't stop." His hand started to trail lower with each word. "I want you screaming my name over and over."

"Cosmos," Sonia panted, her voice breaking.

"Yes, Sonia, just like that and just when you think you've had enough." He paused for effect and Sonia held her breath. "I'm going to make you come again."

Sonia couldn't breathe, this man was dangerous but she was addicted. Her body was on total meltdown for him and now that he had started that ache she fully expected him to help her deal with it.

"Cosmos… I…"

Sonia felt Cosmos go taught, every muscle tensed and in turn her heckles started to rise as she turned slightly and looked up at Cosmos' face. His own gaze was focused on the window, his voice had gone from a sexual husk to a hard growl.

"Sonia, I need you to go back upstairs to the bedroom."

"Cosmos, what is it?" Sonia went to look out of the window but was stopped as Cosmos turned her around in his arms. His emerald eyes blazed with that golden glow but unlike last time it wasn't lust that had caused it. He was now the warrior again from the mosaic, all lethal muscle ready to protect her. She could see that need in his eyes.

"Please, my love, go upstairs and lock the door. Do not come out until I come for you." He cupped her face in his hands and placed a bittersweet kiss on her lips "Sonia, you are my world now," his voice held so much emotion. "No matter what happens I love you." He smiled once more.

"Go on, hellcat"

Sonia felt herself being turned and nudged towards the stairs. A part of her had already figured out that the creatures must have found them and she cursed them. She wanted more time alone with her warrior, the thought that Cosmos would now be going out there to fight them on his own made her nauseous. She didn't doubt his battle skills at all, she just didn't like the thought of him getting hurt for her.

As she reached the top of the stairs Sonia looked down at the man that owned her heart, he stood in only his jeans and was strapping his swords to his back. Sonia couldn't let him go without a final word.

"Cosmos." She waited until he looked up and into her eyes, "Be careful and come back to me. I need my warrior."

He turned and placed a hand over his heart and bowed before he answered, "As you wish, my lady."

Sonia hadn't realised she had been crying until she looked at her reflection when she walked into her room and shut the door. With no lock she pulled her chest of drawers in front and went to curl up on the bed. She hoped with all her being that the battle was quick.

Cosmos flexed his fingers before he walked out of the back door of the cottage. This was what he had been trained for, this was what he knew best. As he stalked around to the front of the cottage he withdrew his swords; breathed in and out deep and slowly. Usually in battle he would only have his own skin to worry about but now he had his Sonia.

He had been hard as rock when she had teased him in the kitchen and he had been ready to teach his wench a lesson in pleasure until he had spotted the creatures in the meadow from the window. Three of them had been stood a few yards apart and they had just watched the cottage almost as if they knew Cosmos would come out and face them. He would beat them, this he knew and had faith in his abilities, he had been trained well and from his time in the mosaic he already had knowledge of what he would face. He had no choice now, the last thing he wanted was for them to get a hold of Sonia. He would lay his life down to protect her. She was his female and an Oracle and to stop these creatures meant he was able to help stop more from coming into this world.

Cosmos could say with a certainty that he no longer thought of killing Sonia and after what they had shared the night before he would rather fall on his own sword than cause her pain. His thoughts flickered back to how responsive she was to his touch and how well his chosen nickname suited her. Every moan she elicited fueled his own desires and he knew he would never tire of touching her even if they had an eternity together.

Cosmos moved through the side gate and out onto the front driveway, his boots crunched against the gravel as he moved he relaxed his wrists then circled them. Loosening his muscles; readying them for the attack. The sunlight flashed as it caught the lethal blades. In the midst of his warm up Cosmos refused to turn and look up at the window. He knew Sonia may be watching — he could feel her gaze on his back and it gave him strength for what he had to do. Cosmos smirked as he prowled into the meadow and towards the creatures, their own forms going into a crouch as they readied for the attack.

"Come on then. Let me send you back to Hades where you belong."

Cosmos moved with a speed unlike any mortal, he was a flurry of steel and lethal ability as he fought to protect his Oracle and love. The three creatures did their part to distract the warrior as the demon, Devastation, creeped into the cottage unseen. Apollo had done his part and had created a hole within the barriers that protected the building and who resided inside. The demon, still in the form of the long dead curator, didn't find difficulty in getting to the Oracle.

Cosmos was unaware of the secondary danger and dispatched the three creatures with ease. His pride soared as he knelt to clean his blades upon the grass, until Sonia's scream rent the air and stopped his heart.

He had failed.

Chapter Thirty-Two

Arianna's scream filled the room as she covered her naked body with the duvet and peaked over the edge to look at the mountain of a man that had appeared out of nowhere in her room. Dressed in black jeans and a black t-shirt he oozed power and masculinity. He currently sported a heavy scowl as he flexed his arms and turned to face the naked form of Arcaeus as he bolted into the room butt naked. Sword lifted ready to do battle, Arianna looked back and forth from one man to the other.

"Arcaeus?" she questioned, unsure what to do.

"Stay under the covers, Anya. Please." Arcaeus lowered his sword and looked back at the imposing male who had now folded his arms and stood waiting, a look of impatience on his face.

"My lord, Hades, to what do we owe this pleasure?" Arcaeus called out and bowed slightly. Arianna thought then that her man would always remain the warrior and for that she would be eternally grateful.

"Hades!" Arianna's eyes widened and she lowered the cover so she could get a better look at one of the elder gods that now stood in her bedroom. "Hades? Wow, no shit. So you are the god of the underworld?"

"Arianna!" Arcaeus' voice boomed through the room as he stalked over and pulled the cover over her head.

Arianna's muffled giggle could be heard, "Oops, sorry."

"Thank you, Arcaeus," the god nodded back. "I am here in Aphrodite's stead. Your old friend, Apollo, has been causing issues."

Arianna heard Arcaeus growl at the mention of the golden god's name, sure as hell that name was able to put her strong warrior into an instant bad mood.

"What has that bastard done now?" Arcaeus again growled out. Arianna would have been intimidated if he hadn't of been naked.

She called out from under the covers, "Arcaeus, my love?"

"Yes Anya?" he called back and she had to once again stifle a giggle.

"Maybe you should get dressed and take our guest into the lounge so I am able to get dressed also."

"Err, yes sorry, you are right. My lord, if you would follow me," Arcaeus' voice turned soft as he did her bidding and she heard them both leave the room. Once she was sure they were no longer present she whipped back the covers and quickly got dressed. She didn't want to miss any of the conversation.

She called out from the bedroom, "Don't you bloody dare discuss anything without me." Arianna quickly jogged into the lounge dressed in yoga pants and a plain blue t-shirt. She stood in the middle of the room and placed her hands on her hips. "Ok, so what's the problem?"

Her eyebrows raised in surprise as the god of the underworld started to laugh.

Arianna then looked at her man and mouthed, "What I say?" Arcaeus just smiled and shrugged his shoulders.

"Aphrodite was right," Hades started to say. "She said being around the mortals was more rewarding and she was right," he smiled and walked into the room more and sat on the end of the sofa. "No wonder she prefers the company of mortals to that of her fellow immortals. Right, shall I start?" Hades looked from Arcaeus and to Arianna, she nodded and tugged Arcaeus to sit on the sofa so she could curl up in his lap.

"So I am sure you are aware the goddess Aphrodite placed certain protection charms over you." Both of the mortals nodded but didn't speak so Hades could continue. "These have now failed and it is one of the reasons I am here, I have been sent to make sure you are ok and that Apollo hasn't tried to visit you."

"Why have they failed?" Arcaeus asked.

"Apollo," Hades said with an edge to his voice. "He has somehow managed to tie Aphrodite's energy and magics to a mosaic and a portal. This portal has opened up a link directly into the deep dark depths of Tartarus and is what brought those creatures you saw here. It also allowed your friend Cosmos to escape as well. Our problem now is the portal is only partially opened and the longer it stays that way the bigger the chance that we could lose Aphrodite forever."

Arianna's voice was quiet compared to the god's, "How did it open in the first place?"

"Your friend, Sonia," Hades calmly stated. "She is the last born Oracle and her blood was what Apollo needed. The issue now is he needs the rest of it to open the portal fully and release the rest of the creatures into your mortal world."

"Fuck," Arcaeus ground out. His hands tightened on Arianna's waist. "How do we stop him?"

"There are only a few options and we are running out of time, but then again so is Apollo. He needs to open the portal by tonight's full moon or else it will close and he will have to attempt the whole ritual from the start."

"But," Arcaeus questioned.

Hades nodded and continued, "As I said, to do this he needs all of Sonia's blood, a sacrifice and the only way we can close the portal permanently is to use Apollo's blood. This will then sever the connection with Tartarus and Aphrodite."

Arianna was stunned. She had thought Apollo would have gotten over being a childish prick since they had last dealt with him but it looked as if he was happy to try and ruin someone else's life as well.

"How in god's name are we to do that then? He's a god for fuck's sake!" Arianna's voice got higher in pitch the more irate she got.

"We beat him by using a god," Hades smiled, his words meaning more to him than to the two mortals. Arianna frowned, "Err, hello. Gods are not allowed to interfere."

Hades just smiled again and nodded towards Arcaeus.

"I will also need your help."

Arianna paled and looked to Arcaeus, her worries etched across her face

"Shh, it's ok, Anya. Let's hear him out, ok? It may not be as bad as you think," Arcaeus motioned for Hades to continue as he held Arianna tighter to him.

"What Apollo is unaware of is who your warrior friend really is."

"Cosmos was always quiet as a child and never mixed much with the other children. Plus, he has gifts that he doesn't tell anyone about. I am assuming Cosmos is the god you are now referring to."

Hades grinned at Arcaeus's quick intellect, "He is a demigod and I don't think he is even aware of it himself. Cosmos has the strength and courage to do what is needed to defeat Apollo."

"If he is strong enough then why do you need Arcaeus?" Arianna questioned, her voice panicked at the thought of her man going back into battle with those creatures.

"Anya, baby, calm down," Arcaeus kissed her head as she wrapped her arms around his neck.

"He is right, Arianna, please calm. I do not want to take him away from you for a battle," Hades smiled and stood. "I will need Arcaeus to go and fetch Cosmos and to deliver him back to the museum where the mosaic is kept and where he will meet his father and end this business." Hades paced as was his way, oblivious to the fact both Arianna and Arcaeus sat shocked at his revelation.

"Apollo has unfortunately moved quicker than I expected and so you must leave immediately,"

Arcaeus nodded and stood, placing Arianna on her feet before he headed into the bedroom to get changed. Hades turned his midnight gaze upon her.

"Your friend, Sonia, has been taken. Arcaeus needs to get to Cosmos as fast as possible so please tell him where her grandma's cottage is."

"Of course," Arianna answered.

"I cannot interfere any more than I already have as much as I wish I could."

Hades bowed low and then vanished in a flash of black and blue, his presence gone as if he had never been.

Chapter Thirty-Three

Cosmos ran full tilt back across the meadow and towards the cottage; swords in hand he vaulted over the back gate.

"SONIA!" he shouted as he stormed into the kitchen, his eyes quick to check each room as he stalked through not wanting to be caught off guard. He made his way quickly towards the stairs taking them two at a time. That one scream had ripped his heart in two and he would deliver a painful death to the one that had forced it from her lips.

Up on the landing he headed straight for her bedroom. Growls and shuffling footsteps echoed and put Cosmos' senses on full alert. He rolled his shoulders and cracked his neck from side to side in an effort to stop the nerves from taking over. He dreaded what he would see, visions of his hellcat mortal wounded repeated in his mind. As he stepped into the doorway he looked to see Sonia's limp form thrown over the shoulder of the creature, but this was the one Cosmos had seen from the window in Sonia's home. Cosmos growled as he looked at his lover's face, it now sported a large purple bruise and multiple scratches from her abuser. Cosmos's rage began to build.

"You will pay for hurting her, demon."

The creature turned its head and its blood red eyes upon the warrior.

"I think not half-breed." Its borrowed form of the mortal melted away and revealed its true likeness, Cosmos moved to enter the room and attack, wanting nothing more than to split the bastard in two and get its clawed hands away from his woman, his fury erupted as the demon looked Cosmos in the eye and ran said clawed hand across Sonia's buttock. As he stepped forward he hit a solid barrier and cried out as his fists hit the solid wall of nothing repeatedly — his hands quickly becoming bloodied. His cries of anger were answered by a throaty chuckle from the demon.

"Pitiful half-breed." The demon turned and faced the far wall where a golden portal opened the demon stepped through and gave Cosmos a glimpse of Sonia's workshop where the mosaic was kept before it closed leaving Cosmos to beat against the barrier.

Cosmos let the fury flow through him as he continued to pound the wall long after they had left. He swore then and there he would find that demon and make him hurt, would rip him limb from limb. Nothing on this earth would keep him from Sonia, not even the gods. With one last strike at the wall he collected his swords and turned around to stalk back downstairs. His thoughts now centred on and around that demon, he would take it apart piece by piece, delivering maximum pain for every bruise it had placed on Sonia's body.

Half-breed! That had stuck in his mind but it set off a round of questions in his head, ones that he had been asking himself since he was young and when his mother was alive. Questions like who his father was? Why was he different? How was he able to heal fast and heal others? But right now he needed a way to get to Sonia and he was drawing a blank. He was stuck in the middle of nowhere and with no ability to call for help. Cosmos felt frustrated that he had no idea of anything in this modern world. Cosmos walked back out into the front meadow to the sound of a horn blaring in the distance. He shielded his eyes as he watched the long curving driveway.

A streak of silver caught his eye and he continued to watch as a silver metal beast screeched to a stop in front of him. Cosmos eyed it warily and reached to grab the hilt of one of his swords when a familiar shout stopped him.

"Cosmos, my friend, stand down." Arcaeus climbed out of the beast and leant his forearms upon the roof.

"Arcaeus, what in the name of Zeus are you doing here? Not that I'm ungrateful."

Arcaeus grinned and motioned for Cosmos to get in, he groaned hoping he would be able to handle another ride inside. Cosmos opened the door and slid into the seat and eyed the interior and then a grinning Arcaeus.

"Buckle up, we haven't got much time. Your father is ahead of us."

"What the fuck are you talking about?" Cosmos ground out. "I don't even know who my father is."

Arcaeus face looked shocked as he turned to face the front and started the car.

"Shit, I thought you knew already. Let's get going and I will tell you what I know."

Cosmos nodded and reached up to grab the strap.

"You will tell me everything, my friend."

"Arcaeus, this machine can move fast, yes?"

Arcaeus smirked, "Oh fuck, yes." He threw it into gear and peeled away from the cottage.

Cosmos' voice filled the car, "Now tell me about my father."

Chapter Thirty-Four

Sonia's cheek throbbed and so did her head for that matter, served her right for not listening to Cosmos and opening that damn door thinking her friend and boss needed her help. As she thought back to what had happened it was so obvious it was a trap Sonia felt stupid that she had fallen for it… She had opened the door thinking it was her friend only to be met by blood red eyes and a clawed hand to her throat. She had screamed her loudest in the hopes that Cosmos could hear her and come to her rescue but after he had tightened his hand she wasn't able to make a sound. She had clawed at his hand in an attempt to get free but then had resorted to nailing him in the balls with her knee. That had earned a smack to the face and a ticket to unconsciousness.

Sonia opened her eyes and looked about in slow movements, anything faster and she thought she would throw up. She was back in her workshop and she was currently tied against one of the boiler pipes in the corner of the room. The mosaic sat in place in the centre of the room. This time, though, Sonia was able to see the surface pulse and ripple as the portal drew in energy. Yes, she figured it was a portal, to where she just didn't know.

"Ahhh, finally you are awake." Sonia was hit with the sense of d jà vu and she remembered the vision only this time it would be different.

As expected a gorgeous man dressed in gold approached. It started to play out just like she expected and she knew what was coming.

"Fuck you," she grated out, her throat felt like she had swallowed razor blades. The male's laugh filled the room, though she had no clue what was funny about her words.

"I think not," he sneered. "If I had more time though I would be tempted." He stalked towards her and grinned "You are indeed a lovely creature and I can see why the warrior became smitten with you."

Sonia glared as she pulled on the bonds that held her wrists. She wanted nothing more than to punch the sorry arse in the face.

"Listen, arsehole, I don't know who you are and to be frank I couldn't give a toss, so either get to the point or piss off." Sonia had lied a little. She had already guessed who the male was by his clothing alone. A man that happily dressed himself in a gold style toga either had to be mentally unstable or Apollo, the sun god, though she wouldn't rule the first one out yet. As she had guessed he stepped forward and wrapped his hand around her already bruised throat. She should have known not to piss off a deity.

"You are just as bad as that other mortal bitch." His words penetrated her mind and caused her vision to play back through her head. On reflex Sonia did what she had never done in the vision. She used her full force, lifted her knee and caught Apollo, god of the sun, straight in the balls.

"That's Miss Bitch to you," her voice was hoarse as Apollo released her throat to clutch his groin a pained groan leaving his lips. Sonia continued to struggle with her bonds all the while she kept her gaze on the god. A growl from her left froze her in place, the demon that had knocked her out stalked across the far wall, its clawed hands clenched and unclenched as it walked from one end of the room to the other.

Its guttural voice filled the room, "It's time release them." Its words froze Sonia and she could guess what that meant, her time was up.

"It will be time when I say it's time," Apollo growled as he stood, he lifted his hand as if to smack her and Sonia refused to flinch and met his gaze head on.

"Go on then do it," she egged him. Sonia's shoulders hurt from being wrenched up behind but she stood tall and faced her captor. Apollo growled and lowered his hand, his beautiful face distorted by rage.

"Untie her, Devastation, and bring her to the mosaic."

Apollo walked off towards the stone and Sonia's stomach dropped. This was it, this was her end, and the only thing that she could think of was how she only got one night with Cosmos. Her heart ached at the fact that she would never see his emerald eyes again or hear him call her hellcat again. Sonia's mind had retreated to her happy place as she was untied and led over to the mosaic. Apollo stood opposite with a cruel smirk on his face.

"Spill her blood. Spill all of it and release your brethren," Apollo's voice boomed and Sonia felt claws at her neck. She closed her eyes and remembered her life and her time with Cosmos. She was glad for one thing…

She had loved and been loved even if it was for one day.

Cosmos stayed hidden until the last possible moment, even though every second delayed caused his heart to tear as he watched the abuse delivered to his Sonia. The trip in the car had been a long and uncomfortable one but he had finally found out some answers. Firstly, it turned out that his father was none other than Apollo himself and that also explained his recent dream about his mother. She had been right, in a way he had taken after his father, he was proud and usually got what he wanted but that was where the similarities ended. Cosmos would burn in the deepest pits of Tartarus before he would let himself become anymore like the god.

Cosmos knew now what he had to do to bring this whole ordeal to a swift end, he just hoped Sonia would see it in her heart to forgive him. He would forever burn with the memories of them together, that alone would have to see him through. Arcaeus had been a true friend and warrior; he had travelled faster than any horse to get him here in his Mercedes 300SL, not that he knew what that meant. Arcaeus had been particularly proud of the mental beast. Cosmos had been grateful to his friend and it had hurt to say goodbye once again. He hadn't been able to contain his chuckle when Arianna's voice had boomed throughout the interior. She had been furious that he had left without her and it had taken a while for her to calm down. Cosmos was happy for his friend that he had finally found the peace and love he deserved.

Cosmos was now perched behind a notice board. He had had to clench his fists when he watched his father grab Sonia by the throat, he had also brimmed with pride when she had fought and kicked the god where it counted. He didn't know any other male that deserved that more than him.

"Spill her blood! Spill it all and release your brethren." Cosmos heard his father's words and moved silently from his hiding place, on silent feet he came up behind the demon that held Sonia. If she hadn't of been so damn close Cosmos would have taken the bastard's head clean of its shoulders. He could clearly see it held Sonia by her throat, its claws precariously close to her jugular vein and Cosmos just couldn't risk it. He carefully slid one of his swords across the demons own throat, the lethal edge bit into the skin.

He leant forward and whispered, "I suggest you release her before I slit your throat."

The demon growled in response but didn't let up its hold. Its claws only tightened and caused Sonia to whimper in discomfort.

"Release her," Cosmos ground out. Sonia whimpered louder and the metallic smell of blood filled the air.

"Welcome, warrior," Apollo's voice called out. "You are just in time. I know how much you enjoyed the creatures' company in the mosaic and soon you will have their company once again."

Cosmos growled low and tightened his hold on the sword that was cutting into the demon's throat. Cosmos knew he would have to move quickly and dispatch of the monster in front of him. Once free this creature could and would do more damage than all of the other combined. He would make it quick and hope no damage was done to Sonia in return.

"Tell your lap dog to release the female," he called out to the golden god, the smug look on his face was starting to annoy him.

"No, or how did your female put it? Oh yes, fuck you."

Cosmos snarled as he ran his sword edge slowly across the throat of the demon, deep enough to nearly sever its head.

"How about you go fuck yourself, Father." Cosmos watched as a torrent of black oily blood spilled down. He ignored the god's shocked expression and let the demon's body drop to floor. In one stride he was up behind Sonia and he collected her in his arms. Blood coated the front of her t-shirt from a deep laceration the demon had created as he had fallen to the floor.

"No, you fool," Apollo's voice rang out and then halted as he reacted to Cosmos' announcement of his parentage. The god then paced and produced incoherent ramblings proof once again the god was on the edge of sanity. Cosmos again ignored it and picked up Sonia and moved her as far away from the mosaic as possible.

"Sonia, wake up for me," he asked gently as he laid her down on the floor, his palm instantly going to the wound on her neck and released the only decent gift his father had ever given him.

"Hellcat, open your eyes," he said in a more demanding tone, knowing that tone would cause fire to light in her eyes if she was awake. His heart stalled and then restarted at twice the pace as she slowly opened her eyes and looked up into his own, her hand reached up to cup his cheek.

"Cosmos, I thought I would never see you again."

"Shh, it's ok," Cosmos cooed and tilted his head to kiss her palm. "Everything is going to be ok, I promise." As he continued to heal her his heart burst as she smiled and looked at him with both trust and love. He dropped his voice low so only she could hear.

"I love you, hellcat. I love you with every fibre of my being. If I could I would reach up and take the stars for you." He smiled down at her, "I can't do that but instead I can keep you safe." Cosmos bent his head and pressed his lips to hers his healing ability kicking in sealing the wound, — he now tapped into a new power, one he didn't know he possessed until now. His whispered words caused tears to fall from Sonia's eyes as she realised what he had done and his intent.

"Forgive me, my love." With one last look at her face he stood and turned to face his father.

"I am no fool, Apollo," Cosmos' voice was loud, his own power filled the room as he accepted who he was. "You are for thinking you could get away with this."

"I am a god and I can do what I like and you are not worthy to call yourself my son."

Cosmos stalked around the mosaic and stood finally toe to toe with the man who had sired him, who once upon a time he had thought would be the greatest man on earth, but now, now Cosmos pitied him.

His voice was calm, "You know I've always wanted to know who my father was. My mother always spoke to highly of you. But now I wish I didn't know. So trust me when I say," he let a smirk cross his face, "there would be nothing better to wipe the knowledge from my mind that you are my sire. Acraeus's father taught me what it meant to be a warrior and how to act with courage and integrity — all of the qualities you so obviously don't possess."

"How dare you talk to me like that. I AM A GOD."

Apollo lifted his fist in a feeble attempt at a punch and Cosmos being the seasoned warrior reacted quickly and grabbed his fist in a vice-like hold. Apollo's eyes widened as he realised Cosmos had inherited his immortal strength. Their arms locked in a battle, Cosmos pulled a knife that had been strapped to his back, he used the tip of the blade to slice across both his and the god's arms, instantly drawing a steady stream of blood.

"What are you doing? Release me at once."

"It's simple," Cosmos started to explain as he pulled Apollo towards the mosaic. "We are going to have some quality father-son time."

"No. Are you mad?" Apollo shot back as he fought against Cosmos' hold on his arm. "If you do this you will never be with your mortal again."

Cosmos looked at male who was his father straight in the eye, their blood now dripped steadily to the floor.

"I know and I would choose to save her life over my own any day. This ends now."

Cosmos moved to embrace Apollo, his arms wrapped tightly around his shoulders and pushed them both onto the surface of the mosaic. The painted stone dipped like fluid and then accepted their bodies into his embrace. The surface once again rippled before it finally froze into place an image of two men so alike stood, arms folded, glaring at each other. A golden glow flashed then vanished, sealing the stonework forever.

The link that had diminished the goddess of love severed immediately along with the power Cosmos had used to keep Sonia in place. Her sobs of heart break the only sounds that remained and the aftershocks could be felt by every god on Olympus.

Their Oracle had lost her soulmate.

Chapter Thirty-Five

"Sonnie, you want to come over for tea?" Arianna called from her office to where Sonia stood in the hallway cataloguing a recent delivery of crates.

"No thanks, Anya. I'm going to have a hot bath and an early night."

Sonia pretended to ignore the sigh that left Arianna as she again turned down another night with the loved up couple. She was thankful for what Arianna was trying to do but she just didn't want to spend another night with two people who were so in love they could barely keep their hands off each other. Sonia always smiled and said it was fine but really she was struggling to keep it together. When Sonia was alone she would find it hard to stop the tears from falling. It had only been two weeks — a meagre fourteen days — since Arcaeus and Arianna had found her curled in a ball covered in blood and sobbing. She hadn't returned to her workshop since. She didn't know how it was possible for her heart and soul to hurt as much as it did. She missed Cosmos every second of every day and nothing she did seemed to help. Unless you counted getting shit-faced drunk like she had the first few night after the event. But the hangover hadn't been worth it. His last words to her played over and over in her mind, *I love you with every fiber of my being*. Her heart did a leap every time she imagined him saying those words to her again, but it also broke her each and every time too.

"Sonnie, are you sure you don't want to come round? We are having Chinese."

"Yeah, honey, I'm sure. Listen, I'm all finished up here so I'm going to call it a day, ok?" Sonia walked over and hugged Arianna hard. "Don't worry about me ok? I will be fine."

Arianna smiled and hugged her back before she stepped away.

"I love you Sonnie, lots and lots like jelly tots."

Sonia giggled and walked into the office to collect her keys and handbag, she still hadn't collected her car from her grandma's cottage so she walked the thirty-minute route home and used the time to think, not that she needed to be doing that. This time, though, she pulled her phone out and dialled the number she had been given in a letter the day she arrived home.

"Hello."

Sonia smiled at the voice she loved, "Hey, Grandma."

"Sonia, darling, how is my little Oracle?"

"I'm ok, I guess."

"Sonia, I know it hurts but it will get better."

"You promise?"

"Yes, my darling, trust in your heart, Sonia, it will never steer you wrong."

"Ok…grandma?"

"Yes, honey."

"When will I see you again?"

"One day, Sonia, one day soon. I love you, princess."

"I love you, Grandma, and thank you."

"Always."

Sonia sighed as the connection ended and she slipped the phone back into her handbag. Why was it the one person that could help her understand and deal with all of this had vanished and she could only call her once a week? The walk home was uneventful. She walked inside her flat and dumped her coat and handbag on the sofa, then went into the bathroom to start running her bath. Without pulling back the curtain she reached inside to place the plug in the plughole and then turn on the hot tap. The sounds of hot water hitting the porcelain was followed by a bellowed shout.

"Zeus' balls!" the voice, loud and deep, echoed from behind the curtain, Sonia screamed and grabbed the nearest item and attacked the stranger. She used the loofah as hard as she possibly could. Sonia was petrified and used all of her might to attack. The curtain pulled from its rail and fell down finally showing her intruder.

"Hellcat, stop!" Sonia froze as if she couldn't believe she was hearing his voice. She was scared she would wake up and this would not be real. She finally looked at Cosmos who was now stood in her bathtub naked. She hadn't moved because she was afraid he would vanish.

"Cosmos?"

Sonia watched Cosmos climb out of the tub and walk towards her, she still didn't speak as he reached out to her and tugged the loofah from her hands.

"Cosmos?" she repeated. Tears started to fill her eyes as he stood in front of her.

"Hellcat," he whispered back as he took her face in his hands. "My hellcat." He bent his head and Sonia closed her eyes as their lips touched. She didn't care how, all she cared about was that he was here and alive and in her arms right where he belonged. Everything else forgotten, Sonia let herself get lost in his touch.

The Oracle now had her warrior, her protector, and her soulmate.

Meton bristled with joy, his feathers rippled as he stretched his wings out and watched his goddess regain consciousness. He had great news to deliver and was even happier to relate that the balance had been restored. Things were how they were meant to be and love had again conquered.

"Meton, my friend," her voice, although groggy and hoarse from misuse, was music to the eagle's ears. "All is well?"

The eagle looked down upon his goddess with adoration and proudly stated, "Yes, my lady, all is well."

She smiled once again at her companion and that was all the payment he needed for his duty to his goddess, his lady, his love.

As Aphrodite always said, love always finds a way.

The End.

Or is it……

A Note From Jenn

Soo I hoped you liked my Cosmos and Sonia, they certainly gave me more than a few issues whilst I was writing SoulFate.
Now before I let you in on a secret can I ask if you loved SoulFate as much as I enjoyed writing it please, please leave a review...it's just like giving me a hug hehe.
Now I know you are probably sat there stewing over how Cosmos got out again!!! And I know you most likely have questions flying round your head *Coughs* sorry about that.

I am not mean so I won't leave you in too much suspense. Here is the answer and an introduction to SoulDeath Book 3 in the SoulMate series.
Can you guess who this one is about?

SoulDeath Coming 2017

Acknowledgements

Wow I honestly can't believe I am on novel number two. This past year has been filled with up and downs but I am happy to say the ups have beaten the downs. I have met some amazing people since publishing SoulKiss and I can hand on heart call them all friends.

So Soulkiss will be a year old on the 4th May and the reaction I have received has been overwhelming and the support has been simply amazing.

I want to say a huge thank you to my street team The Raunchy Rebels for putting up with my random rants and questions. You guys are amazing and I couldn't get through half the stuff without knowing I have your support.

There are a few peeps I want to say thank you to for becoming my friend, making me laugh and believing in me. So to Melody Dawn, Crystal Snyder, Lavinia Urban, KM Lowe, KB Mallion, JA Heron, Dawn A Keane those are but a few of the amazing people who have supported me. I know I could actually go on and on with names.

To Mandy of Mandie Moo Book Reviews who has been always there and always honest, your words mean so much.

My PA's Crystal and Yericka, to a girl new to the indie world to know you have two awesome peeps as these, as well as being the best fangirls any author could ask for I can't say thank you enough.

To Kylie Stewart my fabulous narrator for the audio version of SoulKiss, thank you for being there when I was doubting myself and thank you for trusting me with Legend..#Loveit

To the beast aka hubs thank you for always supporting me and helping. I am happy to say "Love Plums" was all his idea

And finally to my fans thank you so much for taking the time to sit and read Soulkiss and Soulfate. Your support means so much to me. Here's to more stories, more laughs and definitely more love.

You know me I always back Aphrodite.

Live, Laugh, Love
Jenn
xx

SoulDeath Sneak Peek

The bright blue shimmering liquid glimmered in the pale light that filled the throne room of Hades immense stone temple. Sconces burst with flame and caused shadows to pulse and then retreat back against the marble columns. Hades himself sat within the quite of the room, slouched into the chair he had one foot that rested upon the knee of the other leg, his elbows stretched out onto the arms of the dais and in his right hand he held a bottle that contained the blue liquid.

Hades god and lord of the Underworld was confused and irritable. For the first time in his long existence he didn't know how to proceed. The bottle he held within his hands was the love potion he had fairly won from Aphrodite herself. But he was loathed to use it, to force someone to feel what they could possibly never feel on their own ate at his soul. The reputation of the Gods was a harsh one, they were known for not caring about anything but themselves, but as with most things in life what had been said wasn't necessarily right. Hades cared, you could say he cared too much and that was in part what caused his current irritability.

He eyes the bottle one more time and then leant his head back against the head rest of his dais and closed his eyes. He would not use the potion but he would have Aphrodite help him herself and if she was to deny him that request he would be forced to use blackmail. He had after all helped bring her back from the brink of death and help the mortals she was so fond of. He had even addressed the balance and helped the warrior Cosmos. The warrior had made he sacrifice and closed the portal his father Apollo had created by using his own blood and that of Apollo. In doing this he sealed the creatures back onto their plain of Tartarus and severed all ties with the goddess and the Oracle.

This alone had earned him a boon and as he had so obviously fallen for the oracle he was protecting Hades had decided to give him the happy ever after most mortals don't get. Hades smirked to himself, he had left Apollo trapped as a sort of penance for his misdeeds and in short causing a bloody uproar. He had messed with the energies of Olympus herself and as such Zeus had vanished in the hopes he could sort the issue.

Hades opened his eyes and looked at the richly decorated ceiling of the temple, an exact replica of the night's sky had been painted, the stars created from crystals sparkled from their constellations. With a heavy sigh he sat up then got to his feet and stretched his muscled form, the dark toga effortlessly hung to his form and showcased his strength.

He would gain the goddesses help and maybe then his heart would finally get what it had been pining for.

Love…even the gods coverted it

Lightning Source UK Ltd.
Milton Keynes UK
UKOW05f1042290117
293088UK00001B/63/P